* Witchy Business *

WITCHY BUSINESS

(The Witch Detectives #1)

by

Eve Paludan and Stuart Sharp

BOOKS BY EVE PALUDAN

SERIES
WITCH DETECTIVES (Eve Paludan and Stuart Sharp)
Witchy Business
Witch and Famous
Witch Way Out (coming soon)

ANGEL DETECTIVES
The Man Who Fell from the Sky

WEREWOLF DETECTIVES
Werewolf Interrupted (coming soon)

J.R. Rain's
BROTHERHOOD OF THE BLADE TRILOGY
by Eve Paludan
Burning
Afterglow
Radiance (coming soon)

Scott Nicholson and J.R. Rain's
GHOST FILES
Ghost Fire

RANCH LOVERS ROMANCE
Taking Back Tara
Tara Takes Christmas

SINGLE TITLES
Letters from David
Finding Jessie
Chasing Broadway

BOOKS BY STUART SHARP

Court of Dreams

The characters and events portrayed in this book are fictitious. Any similarity to real persons, living or dead, is coincidental and not intended by the author.

Text copyright © 2013 Eve Paludan
All rights reserved.
Printed in the United States of America.

Published by Eve Paludan

ISBN-13: 978-1490412436
ISBN-10: 1490412433

Cover design: David H. Doucot
Editors: Tracy Seybold and Phoebe Moore West

Acknowledgments

My heartfelt thanks go to J.R. Rain for your energetic inspiration, encouragement and enthusiasm.

Stuart Sharp, thank you for your hard work as creator of the first book in The Witch Detectives series. I had so much fun with this collaboration. It is my honor and privilege to work with an author of your talent, caliber, credentials, and work ethic. — *Eve Paludan*

Note

Creative license was taken with the subplot about a certain artwork by a famous artist. So, please suspend your disbelief and just imagine...*what if.* — Eve Paludan

Contents

* Chapter One *

"What does your heart tell you?"
— Samantha Moon in *Moon Dance*

"You look like something the werewolf dragged in," said Rebecca.

"Very funny!" I replied, brushing off clumps of bloody wolf hair from my filthy jeans and quilted bush jacket.

Rebecca was my liaison with the coven who kept me supplied with investigation jobs that utilized my unique talents. She leaned in and plucked a dead leaf from my hair then tossed it in the wastebasket by her desk. "It looks like you had quite the night camping out in the Highlands."

"It was a dirty job, but someone had to do it."

"I'm very impressed that you solved the case of the missing werewolf and got the ball rolling on an agreement to settle."

"It's all taken care of, Rebecca. I got Ferguson Black's statement and gave the edited version of it to the insurers. I got the victim's statement, too. It's dealt with."

"This was your first case involving a werewolf. Did Ferguson Black try to put the bite on you?"

I laughed. "Absolutely not." Mostly because I'd used my talents to ensure that he didn't. "By the time I finally found poor Fergie, he was lying in a ditch, covered in blood."

"*His* blood?" The note of suspicion in Rebecca's voice was typical. Part of her job was keeping an eye out for those supernatural beings who were potentially dangerous.

"Of course it was his blood. He'd just been in a car accident." Actually, Fergie had been so relieved to see me that—even stuck in his wolf form—he'd just wagged his tail and whined. I'd told him who I was and that I was there to help. After he'd finished licking my hands, I'd called in the Highland rescue service.

"You still haven't said how you ended up looking like…that," Rebecca said with obvious distaste.

"Because the weather was so bad last night, the rescue chopper couldn't come right away, and I didn't want them there before I could help Fergie to transform, anyway. We had to hunker down while the sky drizzled on us for the night."

"That explains the bad hair day and your wet doggy odor."

"Rebecca!"

"*Mea culpa.* So, what did you do with him all that time?" That question came with a smirk. Since when did Rebecca have a mischievous edge?

"He was too big for me to carry out of there and his leg was badly broken, so I just worked on keeping him calm until after the moon set and he could transform again. As you may imagine, that was where the conversation paused for a bit."

That was mostly because werewolves' clothes didn't transform with them as they changed, leaving me to spend the night in a ditch with a naked Scotsman.

"I can imagine," Rebecca said.

"I got to watch him transform, though."

"Ah, a learning experience."

I shrugged. "You could put it like that. I didn't know if I should run away or get out my iPad."

Rebecca leaned forward. "*Did* you get any photos?"

"No! I was just kidding about getting out my iPad. That would have been...rude. I mean, yes, I'd saved him, but to video him?"

"I was thinking it might tell us more about the process," Rebecca said. "How it works, what happens to the clothes. There's too much we don't know."

That was the other part of Rebecca's job, scouring my reports for details to take back to the coven. I wasn't sure but the odds were that either Fergie's clothes hadn't survived the transformation, or he'd torn them off afterward. I did know that things had been pretty embarrassing for a moment or two when the rescue chopper came.

"So, you spent the night next to a naked man," Rebecca said. "Did anything happen I should know about?"

"Hardly." I shook my head. Mostly Fergie and I had just talked. About what he was doing out there, about his work as a solicitor up in Thurso. I guessed that another woman might have been tempted by him. I'd just lent him my jacket to keep off the cold. "He was kind of sweet."

"He was an idiot, going out driving when he knew the moon was rising. What did he think would happen?"

"His elderly mother had phoned, saying she had fallen and couldn't get up. What was he supposed to do?" I countered. "He was trying to race to her house before the moon rose. He just didn't quite make it."

Rebecca sighed. "Causing a pile-up in the process. We're just lucky you were there to contain it."

3

"And that he wasn't more seriously hurt. He could have been killed."

"But, Elle, werewolves don't die, except from silver. And all that running about in the wilds...honestly, there are days when I wish supernatural creatures would *think* more."

"On *some* level, he was thinking. He got away from the accident and made sure no one found him. And after he transformed back into a man, he called his sister on my cell to go get their mother off the floor." I paused. "I'm sure glad that I'm a witch and not a werewolf. I mean, they can't control their powers."

"I know. But we do take care of them under our tolerance directive."

I nodded. "It's a good directive of the coven." One I might have voted for, if I were high up enough in it to have a say in such decisions.

"Elle, are you positive that nothing about this case will be getting out? Publicly, I mean?" Rebecca asked, the way she'd asked practically every time I'd finished a job for the coven.

Then again, as my liaison with them, it was kind of her job to dog my steps and ensure that the details were contained. We didn't want normal humans to find out more than they should, now did we?

"No one else was hurt, the payout is arranged, and no one saw anything that they weren't already explaining away for themselves by the time I got there."

"That's good news."

"As always, my lips are sealed, Rebecca." A yawn escaped me. "Sorry, I've been up all night and all morning."

"You're taking the rest of the day off?"

"Please." I didn't actually have to ask her. The coven was my main source of jobs, but not my full-time employer.

Besides, after a day and a half trekking through woodland and heather, a hot bath and a nap was about all that I felt up to.

"I am impressed with the way you took care of every detail," Rebecca said with a smile. It was a politician's smile, but a friendly one. Anyone working for the coven for long enough ended up with a smile like that. That was just the way Rebecca was. If she wanted to get close to you, it was because she had an agenda, but it didn't mean she wasn't being genuinely friendly, too.

Her personality worked with the rest of her: she was always so professionally dressed. Today, she towered over me in her heels and a tailored pants suit. Rebecca was always powdered and perfumed, plucked and waxed, if not Botoxed—she could have graced the cover of any fashion magazine with a little airbrushing around the corners of her eyes. She was right at home wearing haute couture. I had to work a little harder at finding my middle ground between fashionable and comfortable.

She had a point, though, about the effect that I had on clients. Calmness was the commodity that I gave the coven, from my desk at home that served as my little office in Edinburgh, not too far from the castle. Calmness and occasional answers. After all, what else was an enchantress for?

Yes, I was an enchantress, a witch specializing in the manipulation and sensing of emotions. No, I couldn't read minds, and I couldn't produce love potions. Indeed, the list of things I couldn't do was a lot longer than the list of things I could. I was not a diviner or a battle witch, a ritual weaver or an expert in producing focuses. As an enchantress, I couldn't even cast spells, not really.

What I *could* do was influence emotions just enough to, for example, stop a werewolf who had been recently hit by a car from tearing me apart in a fit of pain-fueled rage.

In my line of work, I was also adept at persuading someone who was already feeling guilty that they might want to confess something to me. I could even feel their emotions directly if I concentrated hard enough. I really couldn't read minds, but it had given me a small edge when it came to my day job in insurance investigation. It had been enough, most of the time.

"You should go home," Rebecca suggested. "You look—"

"Like something the werewolf dragged in. I know, you told me." I sighed, because I knew how we must look side by side, right then.

With her being so tall and blonde and professional, and me...well, I looked exactly like someone who had been hiking in the mountains, and tracking down a wounded werewolf, right down to the mud stains covering my jeans and jacket. My hair was currently a tangled, reddish mess and my skin was chapped to within an inch of its life. There were reasons that I normally preferred city life.

"Don't worry," Rebecca insisted. "Somehow, you always manage to look beautiful. Even after rolling around in a muddy ditch with a werewolf and showing up with drool on your clothes."

"At least no one got eaten."

That got a smile from her. Good. It was always nice to make people feel better. Especially her. We weren't exactly friends, but we were friendly. Rebecca moved in different circles in the coven than I did, so any contact we had was generally about jobs that I did for the coven. Their jobs were one of the major reasons I was here in Edinburgh.

Although not the only one, by a long way. Actually, there were plenty of reasons to have my investigation business in Edinburgh. I couldn't think of a better place for a thirtysomething enchantress about town to live than Scotland's capital. Edinburgh was less industrial than Glasgow or Aberdeen, less obvious than London. Perfect in so many ways.

My city was filled with all the life you'd expect from one of the world's great cities, and also, handily, the center of a pretty big insurance trade that let me earn my living in relative comfort. Not to mention my income kept me supplied with DVDs of seasons of *Bewitched*. A girl has to have at least one vice.

Occasionally, I took some of the money I'd earned and went off on holiday somewhere exotic. Last year, I had gone to Santorini for two weeks. Alone, of course. Perhaps ironically, I didn't have that many witch friends. Even *they* sometimes had trouble with the idea that I really *wasn't* able to steal secrets out of their heads.

Greece was nice, even if I did have to keep away from the clubs while I was there. But Scotland was my home and I loved it here, too. Between the tourists and the locals, Edinburgh was always so full of movement and emotion…too full, some days.

I yawned again in front of Rebecca. "Sorry, the job was grueling and I think I might have a few fleas from the werewolf crawling up my leg."

"Where would Fergie pick up fleas?"

"He must have rolled in something dead before I got there."

"Ugh!" I could feel Rebecca's disgust at that one from here. She reached out to put a hand on my shoulder. "Go home, Elle. Take a bubble bath. Scrub yourself!"

I laughed. "That sounds so good right now."

"Go. Your fee will be deposited in your account as usual."

Aching for a bath and rest, I headed home, walking through the city center. The walking route back from Rebecca's swanky Edinburgh office took me past a few of the more avant-garde bars and chic comedy club venues. With each one I passed, I could feel the backwash of emotion emanating from the open doors.

I didn't even try to go inside any of these interesting places, and not just because the bouncers wouldn't let me in looking like I did, covered in mud and with twigs in my hair and fleas crawling up my legs. I didn't go in because too much emotion was dangerous, a sensory overload, like sitting in the middle of the mosh pit at a thrash gig, trying to carry on a normal conversation.

Even in my own life, knowing when to back away was a must. Boyfriends tended not to last very long around me. I didn't even make that many real friends. It was just the price of what I was. All of my teachers had told me that. True enchantresses were rare. I was the genuine article.

Home was an end terrace house that was deeper than it was wide, with a good view out over the city from the upper floors. From outside, it didn't look like much. Inside, it was home. It had been for years. It was comfortable and welcoming, even if I tried not to keep too much clutter in my life. There were fine art prints on the walls and a couple of mementoes from trips spent looking to recover items for insurers.

Home at last, I was ravenous. My kitchen was small but well stocked. I grabbed a glass of buttermilk and poked a wide straw in it. Some of it I drank and the rest would go on my face, as a natural skin treatment. I rumbled through my herb cabinet and got out a blue-glass bottle of pennyroyal oil.

It would thwart any remaining fleas. I peeled off all of my clothes in the utility room and threw them in the stacked washer-dryer combo.

I headed upstairs and showered, running the water as hot as I could stand it, the steamy heat finally making me feel like myself again as I washed the dirt from my hair, several times, until the water ran clear, and conditioned the tangles from my hair. I combed through it while standing there dripping. And then, I took a glorious minty bubble bath with another splash of pennyroyal to ward off or kill any remaining fleas I had caught from poor Fergie.

Even having only known him a few hours, I could see that he was such a mess, as both a man and a werewolf. His mother ruled him, and his werewolf transformations seemed to run his life. From the way he'd talked about Thurso, he hated his job, too. Fergie was really on a downslide. His chagrin at his own life was a reminder of how lucky I was to have the life I had.

The part I didn't tell Rebecca was that Fergie and I quickly got along like old chums and he had even asked me on a coffee date after he got out of the hospital. I had politely declined, the way I so often did, saying that I wasn't allowed to date anyone whose case I was investigating, that it would be unethical. The truth was simpler. There was no emotional spark between us. I wanted a mate, a partner who excited me.

But Fergie? After his injury was attended to and the near-debacle with the insurance company faded, I thought he would make a good platonic friend. I'd seen him at his very worst and he was direct in his communication, humble when he needed to be, and down to earth. With Fergie, there was no arrogance or pretense. What you saw was what you got. There was no façade about him, only this effusive need to be liked that was, after all, rather canine.

Of course, *dating* was always kind of a problem, given that I was meant to keep *away* from strong emotions. Oh, I'd dated. There had been men in my life from time to time. But either I'd just never connected emotionally, which was a deal breaker for me, or a month or two of me knowing everything they felt was too much. As for sex…well, when I spent my life keeping away from strong emotions, that could be an even bigger problem.

I dried off and wrapped in a towel. I headed up to my bedroom. The bedroom was one of the reasons I loved being home. It was as large as the plan of the house would allow, and my big bed filled most of it. Thanks to the stresses of constantly blocking out the world, I liked to sleep with at least seven pillows. My friends had sometimes made fun of me for that when we had sleepovers in our school days.

At thirty-five, without half those friends, I missed that. We'd grown up, drifted apart. Some of the witches among them might have ended up working directly for the coven. More would just be out there living normal lives, their only reminders of the coven's existence coming with the magic they hid from the world, or the occasional tithes to the coven's coffers.

As for the rest of the bedroom, the Georgian wardrobe toward the back was big enough that people could get lost in it if they weren't careful. It wasn't that I had that many clothes. It just seemed to be sort of a bottomless hollow—no matter how many clothes I shoved in there, the wardrobe never seemed to fill up. Someone had once joked that if I went inside, there would probably be a lion in there, as the witch and the wardrobe were already accounted for.

I kept important things like my cell phone, my hair straightener, and my collection of aromatherapy candles in a small dressing table. I loved candles. They could change the whole emotional atmosphere of a room. I made them often and gave them for gifts. Oh, and there was the old photograph of my mother, back before the accident, with a couple of other members of the coven's higher echelons, including Rebecca, who never seemed to age.

There was also a full-length mirror that I stood in front of, trying to work out what to wear. More casual jeans, or did I feel like being the professional me for the rest of the day? I guessed that depended on what I planned on doing. Working, or finally taking some much needed time off? Things had been pretty busy lately. Sleep! Oh, I loved sleep, but the day was so beautiful I hated to waste it. Maybe I would go to the Royal Botanic Garden and look around the glass houses.

Even dressed in a towel, I looked more like myself in the mirror now that I'd showered. My skin was back to its oh-so-pale best that sometimes made people wonder what foundation I was using, my hair had that reddish auburn luster that didn't seem quite so out of place in Scotland, and the sharpness of my features framed eyes that seemed to shift and change color between green and gray, depending on the light.

On the whole, probably thanks to all that exercise I'd been getting chasing after apologetic werewolves, I thought I was doing pretty well for thirty-five years old. Not in witch years, ha—that joke was quite old.

My phone rang, dragging me from my thoughts. I answered the phone, pulling on some underwear as I did and almost going sprawling as a result.

"Elle Chambers," I said a little breathlessly as I got my balance.

"Ms. Chambers, this is Iain Peach from Gerard and Philips." The accent was softly Shetlands, as if its owner had tried hard to lose it as he'd gone up in the world. If he was working for G&P, he *had* gone up in the world. They were one of the firms I occasionally consulted for, and they weren't the sort of company that most people contacted for home and contents or health coverage. G&P were specialists.

"Something rare has been stolen," I said.

"How did you know that?" he asked.

"Magic."

"This really isn't—"

I sighed. "You specialize in insuring high-value objects. I can hear how worried you are, and G&P have used me when things have gone missing previously." So...not magic at all. Face to face, I couldn't have read his mind. On a phone, I couldn't even pick up emotions, beyond hearing nice insurance brokers sounding like they were about to have some kind of breakdown. "You sound very upset. What's happened?"

"About an hour ago, we received a call from one of our customers notifying us of a potential claim relating to an insured item."

Trust an insurer not to get to the point. "And the item is?"

"A rare M.C. Escher. We believe it to be the only one in existence."

That made it valuable. One of the side effects of my job was that I had to keep up with prices for these things. An ordinary print of one of Escher's designs might not make more than a few hundred dollars on the international market. A rare one could be worth a hundred thousand. Not the biggest payout G&P had ever made, but certainly one worth calling me in for.

Why? Because I could save them money. First, I'd check whether the claim was real. Then, if I could, I'd try to recover the item. Even if it meant buying it back, that wouldn't be at the full insured cost. In the absolute worst-case scenario, where the insurers made a final payout before I found it, at least they'd have the art to defray the cost. This was all assuming I could find it, of course, but my record was as good as anyone's.

"So," I said, "where will I have to fly to? Which museum?"

"It isn't a museum," Iain replied. "The client is a private collector."

Private collections were a little rarer than they used to be, at least outside of bank vaults. Nowadays, a buyer at an auction was as likely to be someone like Iain's bosses, buying a valuable investment, as it was someone just wanting to put it up on a wall.

"Even so, I'd better get the tickets booked," I insisted, trying to remember where in the house I left my laptop.

"You won't need to fly," Iain said quickly. "Actually, that's part of the reason we're contacting you about this one. The theft occurred in Edinburgh, in the home of one of our clients, Niall Sampson. If you're interested, I'll email you the details. We'd appreciate it if you could get started straight away. Mr. Sampson is quite anxious that this be dealt with quickly."

Was I interested? I didn't need to think before I answered that. What else was I going to do? Go out and acquire a social life in all those bars I didn't dare step inside? Call Rebecca and see if she had any more cases out in the middle of nowhere for me to take? I might not have been able to enjoy everything about the city, but the chance to look for stolen art in the middle of the city I called home? That was everything I could wish for right now.

"I'll get over there straight away," I said. "My usual terms?"

"Of course." There was a pause as Iain cleared his throat. "The item in question is going to cost G&P about £1,000,000 if we have to pay off the claim to the client. So, your ten percent fee for this job, if you recover the Escher, would be—"

"£100,000?" About thirty percent more than I had budgeted for the total value of the rarest Eschers, given the exchange rate. What had he produced that was worth that? I struggled to keep my voice calm. "Of course."

Iain sighed heavily. "Find it."

There was one good thing to come out of all this: at least I now knew which outfit I was going to wear for the rest of the day.

* Chapter Two *

The outfit in question consisted of a dark skirt, cream blouse and dark jacket, with comfortable stacked heels that were just high enough to be noticeable but just low enough that I could walk anywhere with them, even in a garden. An old, but still serviceable, Gladstone bag contained my laptop, along with everything else I might conceivably need for an investigation. Which meant I could quite happily use the bag as a blunt instrument, or possibly an anchor, if it came down to it.

Even so, I barely felt dressed up enough for the house where Iain's directions led me. A large Georgian townhouse sat surrounded by a waist-high stone wall—it was the kind of place that only the city's richest inhabitants could possibly afford. Of course, I should have guessed that part already. G&P's clients weren't exactly poor, as a rule.

I pulled my car up in front of the place, behind a police forensics van and a couple of squad cars. There was a uniformed officer waiting discreetly by the front door. He looked around restlessly, as if they were just finishing up, which meant that they'd obviously been sent here straight away, had done their investigation, and were ready to go either for a late lunch or on another call. It was either efficiency at its best, or someone didn't care as much about the crime as they should.

My initial thought was that it was probably efficiency. Contrary to what people saw on TV, the police were usually pretty good at their jobs. The only problem they faced was one of resources. Like forensic hours. That the forensics van had been sent at all was actually quite impressive. Most people who got burgled were lucky to get any kind of forensics at all, let alone a couple of hours after the crime. Apparently, the theft of something as expensive as the rare artwork made it as much of a priority as murders or drug traffickers.

The local police reaction to this theft potentially made things quite interesting for me. The attitude of the police to my work varied considerably, from the officers who didn't want me anywhere near their crime scenes, to ones who accepted that I was potentially a valuable asset and a source of information. Which I was, generally, so long as that information didn't involve too many things that the police weren't meant to know about.

Like exactly how I got my results. Around police officers and detectives, I had to remember not to do anything too overt with my powers. It would not do to let the Lothian and Borders police force start worrying about witches. Not only did Scotland have some unhappy history where we were concerned, but it would also mean giving away the secret of my biggest advantage.

I took out my business card as I approached the officer on the door.

"Good afternoon. I'm Elle Chambers. I've been assigned to look into this theft case for G&P Insurance. May I go in?"

The officer gave me a look that suggested he had probably been told to keep the general public out, but wasn't sure how that applied to insurance investigators. I made the decision easier with the smallest push of my power. Not much. Just a little tendril of general good feeling.

I smiled without teeth showing, yet exuded a pleasant friendliness that definitely set boundaries as a professional colleague.

"I'm expected."

That assertive statement hit the mark, because the officer smiled back. "Yes, ma'am. We're almost done here anyway."

That meant that either things were open and shut, or there hadn't been too much to find. Either way, it meant that I probably wouldn't have to worry about there being too many police around while I worked. Or about having to do things their way.

I went inside—the inside of the house was so opulent it almost took my breath away. Thanks to a few years of going after expensive items, I did manage to refrain from oohing and aahing. The décor matched the outside, and there wasn't one stick of modern furniture. Everything was antique, and probably expensive to boot. Certainly, I spotted plenty of Chippendale and Charles Rennie Mackintosh as I went through the hallway. It might have been easy to get lost in a house like that, but I could feel the pull of a cluster of emotions ahead of me, so I set off toward them.

That snooping quickly brought me to a room that was more like a museum gallery than anything most people would keep in their homes. There were original paintings hanging from the walls, all expensively framed, and the lighting was every bit as fitting as a museum's. I spotted a Hogarth and a seventeenth-century work by Gabriel Metsu. Sculptures stood on marble and obsidian plinths, mostly complex, modern pieces whose appearances seemed to change, depending on the angle from which the viewers looked at them. It was a stunning room, obviously created by an art collector who loved his pieces and treated them as precious children.

There was not a speck of dust anywhere.

At the heart of it all was an empty space on the wall. There was nothing as jarring as the space where a picture used to hang. Not just an empty space, but a definite absence, in the noticeable fading of the wall paint around it, and in the asymmetry the absence created in the spacing of the pictures around it. It was impossible to ignore. Around the empty frame shape in the paint stood three people: a police detective in his fifties making notes, a younger woman in the coveralls of a forensics specialist, and…

I knew he had to be the owner of the house the moment I saw him. No one in the police would dress quite so elegantly, in dark navy pants, a crisp white shirt with silver art deco cufflinks, and a waistcoat. It made him look a little like he'd just stepped in from a formal function, or maybe just from another era.

It wasn't just the way he was dressed, though. He was…handsome was the wrong word. This man was beautiful in a way that suggested he should have been in one of the paintings on his walls, not just admiring them. His blond hair fell loose almost to his shoulders, and the shape and stance of his body hinted that beneath those clothes he was fit and athletic, while his features were simply astonishing. He had to be at least my age, but there was something about him that seemed almost ageless. I only realized that I was staring when it occurred to me that the only way I could know just how deeply blue his eyes were would be if he were looking straight at me.

"Um…I'm Elle," I managed, and then tried to recover a little. "Elle Chambers. I'm the insurance investigator from G&P."

"It's a pleasure to meet you, Elle," he said, extending a hand. There was a slight accent to his speech that I couldn't place, though it was subtle and attractive. His touch was soft, almost sensual. I had to push back the urge to swallow nervously when his eyes flickered over me, measuring me, contemplating me. As for the urge to reach out and check what he felt in that moment…no. I wasn't sure I wanted to know.

"I'm Niall Sampson. This is Detective Inspector McAndrew."

I was embarrassed when the police detective looked me over too, but at least with him, it was professional. Actually, it was *totally* professional, which was kind of a new experience for me. Even the PC on the door had been checking me out a little. This one was simply a little suspicious.

"Good luck getting anything out of this one," he said. I took the grumbling as a sign that I'd met whatever standard he had to count as a colleague of sorts. "We've interviewed all the staff. We've checked for forensics. So far, nothing."

"So, I might as well go home?" I suggested with a smile and a tiny push of my talent at the detective.

"I didn't say that," DI McAndrew replied. "Though I'm sure you've got better things to do."

"Better things than trying to do my job?" I shook my head. "I'm sure you'll understand if I at least try before giving up?"

"I have every faith that you'll find my Escher," Niall said then, turning his eyes from DI McAndrew to me. "You have quite a reputation, Ms. Chambers."

Why did I feel slightly disappointed that he hadn't called me Elle again? I tried to focus on the job.

"Can you tell me anything that might help our investigation?" I asked DI McAndrew, carefully getting back into his territory.

"Like I said, nothing. No fingerprints are out of place, so far. Only staff and Mr. Sampson. No obvious damage on entry. We'll keep the file open, in case someone is stupid enough to try to sell the piece, but until then…well, give us a call if you discover anything." McAndrew handed me his business card.

It was as good as saying that I was on my own. Until I found something, they wouldn't be throwing effort at a case where there didn't seem to be a chance of a result. The DI and his forensic support left a minute or two after that, leaving Niall and me alone in the gallery room.

"This is a spectacular room," I said, unable to help myself.

"I'm glad you appreciate it. Would you like coffee?" he asked, smiling in a way that made it hard to think.

"Hmm?"

"I assume you'll want to ask me about what happened, Ms. Chambers? Perhaps we could do that over coffee in the living room?"

"Yes, yes, of course," I said, cursing myself for being so slow. What was wrong with me? Was just being around this man enough to do that? There was something different about him, certainly. Something that felt…I couldn't say how it felt, only that I hadn't felt it before. I, of all people, should have been able to label feelings, but not this one.

We walked through to an elegantly furnished room with matched Regency armchairs around a coffee table that looked like it had been brought in from India a hundred years ago. There was a piano in the corner by Wood, Small and Son, at least a hundred years old. A young woman wearing a very plain and businesslike outfit came in to offer us coffee.

"Marie, my assistant," Niall explained.

"I'll want to talk to her," I said, trying to get my mind back on the case, "as well as to any other staff here."

"That would be Kelly, my housekeeper, and David, my driver."

I nodded, taking my cell phone out of my bag. It was as easy to make notes on as a notepad, and I wasn't as likely to lose it. "So, Mr. Sampson—"

"Niall, please."

"Niall, what can you tell me about what happened here? I know you must have been through it with the police, but I'll need to put it in my preliminary report to the insurers, and any detail that you can remember might be important."

"There isn't much to say." He looked over at me apologetically. "I had been out of the house for a few hours at a business meeting. My staff remained behind at home, but they were apparently caught up with their individual jobs, and so didn't go into the collection gallery for several hours. When I got back, I discovered my Escher had been taken. I called the police and my insurers straight away."

I needed more details. "I'll need to hear more about your security arrangements. The make and model of your alarm system, the locks on the doors, and so on."

Niall smiled. "With that, I mostly followed the arrangements the insurance company suggested."

"Mostly?" *Mostly* wasn't a good word when it came to doing things right.

"They wanted me to shut away my collection in a climate-controlled vault."

I looked at him, trying to gauge him. Trying to get a sense of his emotions. The mixture right then was too complex to get a firm grip on, though. "Why didn't you?"

"Beauty locked away in a vault would be only a fraction of what it was meant to be. Can you understand that, Elle? That beauty can only be appreciated if it is truly fulfilling what it is meant to be?"

"Of course."

"This is my home and I like to look at my pieces in a living environment, where I can enjoy them as I wish. Art is about the emotions it produces. There is nothing worse than having a piece of art you have to visit by unlocking a steel door, turning on florescent lights and then standing in a vault to look at it."

"That environment doesn't seem do them justice," I agreed.

"I see you love art, too," Niall remarked.

"But you don't put your art out in a public gallery," I pointed out.

"What can I say?" Niall asked. "I like to enjoy what is mine. A museum, with its opening hours and its restrictions, would make that difficult."

I smiled, knowing that there was a game behind the words, but not wanting to get caught up in it. I had work to do.

"As an art lover, I do respect your position on security. However, as an insurance investigator, well, I would be remiss if I didn't point out that both a vault and a museum would have been more secure."

"Of course, I see your point. Tell me though, Elle, could *you* do that?"

Since I was working for his insurers, there should really only have been one answer to that. Yet, it wouldn't have been the truth, and I got the feeling that not telling the truth would cost me a lot of Niall Sampson's respect.

"I like art where I can look at it," I admitted. "It feels…dead, in a vault. But it's hard to look at when it has been stolen."

Niall shrugged, making the movement somehow graceful. "I was hoping you would be able to help me with that part. The loss of the Escher is a grave blow to my collection. I feel like a child has been kidnapped."

"So, you want me to succeed where the police can't?"

"I suspect that you are capable of far more than they are. Far more than you let yourself believe, maybe."

I didn't know what to make of that. Maybe I *would* be able to do things the police couldn't. I could talk directly to criminals, for one thing. I could act without having to worry about how it would look at a trial, too. As an insurance investigator, I had fewer rules in my way than the police. My employer didn't mind about chains of evidence, as long as cases got solved. So long as they didn't have to pay on the claim, the rest didn't matter so much. And I had my magic. Not that Niall Sampson would know anything about that. Or would he?

"When did you discover the artwork was missing? I mean, all the steps that led up to you noticing that it was gone."

"Right after I came home from my business meeting."

I could picture him, coming home after a stressful meeting, wanting to go to his private collection to unwind. I forced myself to focus. "I have a photograph of the Escher of course, from the insurer. Do you have other photos besides the ones for the policy?"

"I'll have to dig them up and email them to you."

"Thank you." I took a sip of the coffee and held in a groan of pleasure. It was *good* coffee.

23

"What else would you like to know?"

"A little history on the artwork would be nice. I like Escher's graphic design pieces, but I don't know this one."

"It's somewhat…different to his usual work," Niall said.

I looked at him over my coffee mug. "Tell me."

"In 1931 or thereabouts, Escher was illustrating a Dutch horror novel for an acquaintance." He paused, looking at me carefully as he said, "In English, the title is *The Terrible Adventures of Scholastica*—it was about a woman who was accused of witchcraft in the sixteenth century."

I kept my expression deliberately blank and waited for him to go on.

"Back then, one of the methods they used to determine guilt were scales that were used to weigh accused witches. If they failed to weigh in correctly, then they would be killed, usually burned. The scales in the story were, unusually, not rigged. They were honest scales, and in the end, the suspected witch was found innocent."

"I love a happy ending," I said, although I was having a harder time letting nothing show on my face. "So, the Escher is what?"

"Escher made woodcuts that were used to make illustrations for the book, as well as illuminated letters."

I nodded. I'd always enjoyed the richness of those.

Niall kept going. "*The Terrible Adventures of Scholastica* was only printed in Dutch, in a limited edition of 300. There were nineteen or so woodcuts of Escher's for the book. He made at least one woodcut that was never used in the book. The letter A. That was what was stolen from my collection."

"Just that. A print of the letter A?" Being a professional, I didn't point out that it sounded like Sesame Street might be responsible for the crime.

"Not a print," Niall corrected me. "The actual woodcut block Escher made. It is so rare there is not even a print available of the letter. It is a one-of-a-kind artifact."

"Even so, to be insured for a million…" I said, stopping only because I suspected Niall wouldn't like being told that I couldn't see how his precious artwork could possibly be worth the money.

"There is more that is not public about the woodcut block." Niall paused. "I have examined it many times. There are mystical symbols carved into it, so densely that it is hard to read them. There are those who say the woodcut is…magical."

I had a special laugh for those moments when people brought up the idea of magic. One that said *oh, but we don't believe in nonsense like that, do we* as clearly as possible. I deployed it then and Niall looked at me carefully.

"I have one of just 300 original copies of *De vreeselijke avonturen van Scholastica*. I was intrigued enough by the story to set about trying to obtain the illustrations in other forms. I found that I could purchase prints from the book. But not of the letter A, you see?"

"That's why you had to have the wood carving. It's one of a kind."

"Yes. I prize one-of-a-kind things." He shot another smile my way. "I trust you will be discreet with your report to the insurers? All of this…"

"I am very discreet," I assured him. "Trust me, my insurers aren't interested in anything beyond whether I recover a stolen object."

Niall let out a sigh. "That's good."

"Has anyone ever shown interest in the Escher woodcut block? Collectors?"

"Almost no one. It's so obscure that I doubt most people would even understand its value."

He had a point there. "Who knows the history?"

"My staff knows bits and pieces. Perhaps there are scholars who might know of the strange hidden symbols, or the rarity value of the block."

"Who framed it?" I asked, casting around for possible connections to the art world. A framer would often research a piece when he or she worked on it.

"I did it myself."

So much for that. I closed my eyes for a minute. A vague memory of art history came to me. "Who was Escher's mentor?"

"Why?"

"Sometimes, the best way to find something stolen is to find the *reason* it was stolen. Indulge me, Niall."

"Samuel Jessurun de Mesquita was his graphic arts teacher and also was a woodcut artist of many beautiful prints," Niall said. "He died with his wife and son, in Auschwitz."

I swallowed, trying to imagine the horror of that and knowing that I couldn't.

"If Samuel had the block—perhaps as a gift or memento from Escher—that would explain why no prints were ever made from it," I said.

"What an interesting idea. The provenance is…well, *difficult* with that piece," Niall admitted. "Could my woodcut block have been stolen Nazi booty?"

"It's just a theory."

"One that provides us with a possible reason for someone to try to steal it back," Niall said.

I shrugged. "Possibly. Or it could be nothing to do with that. It could just be that someone wanted it, or that they

26

found out what it might be worth. I'd like to believe that it was something more…"

"Romantic?" Niall suggested.

"Worthy of it," I corrected him, "but the truth is that until I find it, we won't know."

"And you will find the woodcut?" Niall asked, reaching out, his fingers just brushing my arm.

I nodded. "You can bet on that. I'm very good at my job."

"Oh, I guessed that," Niall assured me. "You are a true art aficionado and a very interesting insurance investigator. I don't often meet women as clever as you…Elle."

I liked the way he said my name. It sent a wave of warmth through me.

"Thank you. On that note, I should finish my investigation and go back to my office."

He smiled and nodded to a plate at the center of the table. "Yes. You should. Although not before you try the shortbread."

I finished my coffee and tasted it, just to be polite. I finished it with a wide smile on my face. "This is good. You should pass on my compliments to your cook."

Niall shook his head. "This is one small triumph I can call my own."

Okay. *This* man baked? "Thank you, Niall. You are a man of many talents."

"Well, you can't eat art, now, can you?"

I laughed. "You are an amazing baker. Do you make art, too?"

"I do." Niall gestured in a way that seemed to take in the piano, the shortbread, the whole room. "I try to explore all the ways there are to touch the emotions of those around me. So far, my art is not very good, but it pleases me."

"So, is there a room like the other one, a gallery, except filled with only your own art?"

Niall smiled like he might not answer, but then nodded. "There is. Only the staff know of it. And one or two close friends."

That sounded like an invitation. "Maybe another time, after I solve the case of the missing Escher, you'll show me some of your own artwork."

"I'd like that," he said warmly. "Very much so, in fact. Perhaps I will even have to work on some etchings, just so I can say that I have shown you them."

It was an old joke, but the promise behind it seemed real. A thread of joy spiraled through me and I cloaked my reaction carefully, so I could return to being a professional insurance investigator.

"I think I'd better get on with interviewing your staff now," I said, reluctantly standing.

I caught a thread of something that was almost disappointment, coming from Niall, as if I had failed some sort of test by shutting the conversation down like that. Even so, he stood with me. His eyes were latched onto mine and warmth bloomed in my body. Embarrassingly so.

"My staff will offer any assistance you require," he assured me. He opened a drawer of a side table and handed me a business card and uncapped a gorgeous Waterman fountain pen. He turned over the business card and wrote a phone number. His script was very artistic, with grand loops and the European hash mark through the number seven.

"This is my private number. You can contact me anytime. Day or night."

I tried not to think too hard about the images that last word conjured up, of Niall having to get out of bed to answer the cell phone. Would he be wearing paisley silk pajamas and a red velvet smoking jacket? Would he be wearing anything?

"I will call if I find anything to report about your missing Escher," I promised.

I made my way out through the house then, looking for Niall's assistant, finding her in a small library that seemed to double as an office. She was young and dark-haired, very pretty but, as it turned out, completely unable to help me.

"I'm sorry," she said, after I had asked her a few questions. "I feel so stupid, not having seen anything. Mr. Sampson went out for his meeting with the Durham backers, so it was just the three of us—the staff—in the house. I was mostly in here, trying to ensure that some of the contracts were in order, although I might have gone through to the kitchen once or twice for tea. I really didn't notice anything until Mr. Sampson came back and raised the alarm."

My abilities weren't perfect when it came to telling if someone was lying, but it seemed like she was telling the truth. She seemed genuinely upset to have let Niall down by failing to spot the break-in. More than that, I could see how loyal she was to him.

I asked the driver, David, and the housekeeper, Kelly, the same questions. Nobody had seen anything, but they had all gone to the kitchen at some point. Other than that, it seemed like they had all just gone about their normal duties until Niall had gotten back.

Which was a problem, because if they were all telling the truth, that no one saw nor heard a thing related to the theft, then we had a thief who could take a work of art from a secure, alarmed property in broad daylight without anyone noticing. Was that possible? *Maybe.* It was certainly a large enough house that three people could be at different corners of it and never see one another, let alone anyone else. More than that, if they heard someone moving about, they would simply assume that it was one of the others going to the kitchen for a snack.

I left the house still thinking about that, promising to do everything I could. Still thinking about Niall, too, although that was normal, wasn't it? He was a client. I was meant to think about him. Although possibly not the way I did.

Perhaps it was because I was so distracted that I got most of the way home before I realized that someone was following me.

First, it came to me as a prickle on the back of my neck. A tiny certainty that someone's attention was on me. It had probably been there before, but I'd ignored it because I was thinking about Niall. And because it was normal for me, up to a point. I always got a lot of interested looks when I was out and about. Mostly from men. Yet, this prickle didn't go away, the way those generally did.

Finally, I had to start paying attention to it. Thankfully, it was still a busy street in daylight. I slipped into a doorway, waiting as the sensation got closer and closer…

Footsteps came close and I stepped out to confront whoever it was, trying to remember the basics of the self-defense courses I'd taken. If this was some would-be mugger, I wanted to be ready with my skills. Only it wasn't a mugger. Anyone but.

I stared at Rebecca as she stood in front of me. "You scared me half to death, stalking me like a fiend. What are you doing?"

"That," she said, "is almost exactly what I was about to ask you."

* Chapter Three *

When Rebecca grabbed hold of my arm and practically frog-marched me back in the direction of Niall's home, I thought about pulling away, just on general principles. That wouldn't have been a good idea, though. Although she worked as a liaison to the coven, Rebecca was far more of a generalist as a witch than me, giving her far more direct combat magic, even if her primary skills were in ritual and divination.

My witch skills were more in the areas of emotion sensitivity and emotion manipulation. That meant that I could feel, for example, the anger coming off Rebecca as she pulled me along. Great. That made two of us.

"Are we running from the police?" I quipped as I kept up with her frantic pace.

"Worse," she replied, which startled me.

"So, is this a reality show and I'm not privy to the joke? Where are the video cameras?"

"Don't push your luck, Elle. Death would not become you."

Okay, now things were getting interesting. Since when did Rebecca make death threats to get what she wanted? So, I let her lead me, trying to ignore the embarrassment of it all. It was actually quite intriguing to let her pull me around. What was she going to do with me, now that she had my attention? More importantly, what could she possibly want in Niall Sampson's place that she had to try to force me to go back there under a life-or-death edict?

I would have gone to Niall's of my own accord, so there was certainly no need for this head teacher and child routine. As she led me toward Niall's, about the only reason I cooperated was that it seemed so out of character for Rebecca.

Ultimately, though, at the last moment, just when I thought we were about to walk up and knock on Niall's door, she headed across the street. Her fingers dug deep into my flesh, propelling me. This house wasn't quite as large or impressive as Niall's, but it must still have cost a small fortune. An estate agent would have called it the cheapest house on the block, and stressed the exclusivity of the location.

They would have been sensible to do it, too. Although the property was still in the Georgian style, it had the look of a property that had been empty for a while. The front garden, such as it was in a city as crowded as Edinburgh, was overgrown with weeds and old newspapers were piled up like drunken gnomes. A real estate sign that said, "Fix Up" lay ignored by the front steps. There was even a broken window with a spider making a grand web in the missing-glass space between the outdoors and indoors.

"Hello, eensy weensy spider," I said as we passed the creature. She looked at me with all of her eyes and blinked.

"Greetings. I'm moving in with my egg sac," came a thin, high-pitched voice. I should have expected that. Magic spiders. Obviously. This was Scotland. Where else did the story of Robert the Bruce and the spider come from?

"Congratulations," I said to the spider. "I hope it's a girl, and a boy, and a girl, and a—"

"Don't talk to the help," Rebecca admonished me. She breezed up the stairs and pulled me to the door, which was huge and looked halfway to a gothic style, like something out of an old horror movie. It didn't really fit with the architectural tone of the area.

"Nice," I said when I saw the bronze gargoyle door knocker. I lifted the knocker and let it go. An impressive boom sounded, one that reverberated throughout the neighborhood and shook under the soles of my shoes.

"Great special effect," I said. "Did you do that or is the knocker actually designed like that?"

Rebecca didn't answer. Without waiting for someone to come to the door, Rebecca opened it and we went right in as if she owned the place. Maybe she did. Maybe the coven did, at least.

Although if it did, it could have done a better job of furnishing it. I immediately surmised that this place was not really lived in, not in the traditional sense. Although it was probably cheaper to rent it unfurnished, inside, it was almost bare, down to floorboards under my feet, with no sign of any home comforts. No pictures on the walls, no furniture, no lamps, no television. No guy in a mask and a cape playing a huge pipe organ. Nothing but what was built into the house was in evidence.

"Oh, goody. Are we going camping?" I teased Rebecca and nodded at the dark, cold fireplace and the giant hearth in the living room as we trotted past it. "If this is where the coven has you staying now, they should have given you a decorating budget, or at least a sleeping bag, a flashlight and a S'mores kit," I said, trying to defuse some of the tension. "I'll bring the marshmallows and the graham crackers if you bring the chocolate candy bars."

She grunted a reply that I couldn't make out because it sounded like a strangled sob.

"Rebecca, please. None of this makes any sense to me. And you have your shields up so high, I don't know which end of you is up."

I thought about maybe using my emotion talents to make Rebecca calm down enough to stop holding my arm as if she would pull it off if I ran, but the first flicker of power I sent without thinking ran into her shields.

Rebecca looked round at me sharply. "Don't even think about doing that. You've caused enough problems as it is."

"Me? What problems have I caused?" I was getting a little sick of her attitude. Especially when earlier today she'd congratulated me on a job well done. "What's going on, Rebecca? And why do you get to pull me through the streets like I'm some kind of misbehaving kid who is headed for the principal's office for a stern talking-to?"

"Rebecca? You got her?" That deep voice coming from down the hall was innately, completely, male and the timbre of the throatiness sent his words clearly through the empty house.

"So, a giant lives here?" I said. "Fee-fi-foe-fum!" I called and it echoed back at me in the empty hallway she was propelling me through. It seemed like the only possible response when everyone else was being so serious.

"You are absolutely insufferable," Rebecca said.

"Someone has to save you from your...Grimm...outlook on life."

"Oh, do you never stop? Elle, you don't seem to understand the gravity of this situation."

"First of all, Becca, I don't even know what the situation *is*. I figure that the situation is somewhere between you having a bad hair day and an asteroid heading straight for Loch Lomond. So, while I wait for you to tell me your problem, I figure if I can get you to laugh, then you won't feed me to the giant at the end of the hallway."

"Don't call me Becca. I hate nicknames."

"Fine. I didn't know that." *I did.* I figured it was probably the only revenge I was going to get for being dragged down the street.

"There's a lot you don't know," she said ominously.

"Rebecca, do you have her?" the giant voice boomed again. "Is Elle here?"

"Yes. I have her now!" Rebecca shouted and looked hard at me. "Come on. He's waiting."

"You still haven't told me what this is all about. And who is the guy with the theatrical voice? I mean, seriously, he could audition for movie trailer voiceovers. Who is he trying to impress?"

"Stop," Rebecca ordered. "Just stop. This is about what you were doing in Niall Sampson's house, and this is not the moment to argue."

Really? Then when was? "I think this is *exactly* the moment to argue," I insisted. "I was on an important insurance investigation job when you grabbed me. A rare artwork was stolen from the client's home, and I don't have the time right now to spend being pulled around the streets."

Rebecca sighed. "I don't remember referring you to that job through the coven."

Was that what this was about? Rebecca knew I had other sources of jobs besides her. I had even been under the impression that she approved of it. After all, I would often hear about things with a more…unusual angle to them before she did that way. Half the time, I could solve things before she even got involved.

"Is this about the coven's cut of my fee?" I asked. "Because if it is, they'll still get their tithe, the same as always."

"You don't understand, Elle. This isn't about money."

"So, what *is* this about? Enlighten me."

She took a deep breath and let it out, holding back…a lot of her thoughts. I could feel the emotions there, half-occluded behind her shields, whirling.

"Rebecca? A little information, please?"

"I'm trying to save you," she choked out.

"Save me?" I looked hard at her. "From what?"

The man with the oh-so-threatening voice finally stepped out into the hall. I stared. But then again, he was worth staring at. He was well over six feet tall, probably approaching seven feet in stocking feet, more with the studded motorcycle boots he wore. He was dressed in black leather pants with chains hanging from them and a tight, sparkling white T-shirt that did nothing to disguise his muscles. Not that much could have. He was built like a bodybuilder, except that every muscle looked absolutely functional. His dark hair was cropped short, the center raised up high in a gelled rooster style, but it was the tattoos that caught my attention.

Oh, those tattoos!

They spiraled up his arms in interweaving patterns that might have looked vaguely Celtic or tribal to the casual observer, a mix of swirls and knots and spikes that seemed to shift with every movement, like Ray Bradbury's *The Illustrated Man*. My curiosity was piqued. I had heard of living tattoos, of creatures and objects moving and trapped in the skin of a witch or warlock, of power worked directly into flesh, but had never seen them before. I was mesmerized by his tattoos and how they moved and writhed on his skin. I was pretty sure my mouth dropped open a bit. I slammed it shut so I wouldn't look like a teenage witch.

I could feel the power there and I spotted some familiar shapes among the patterns, sigils that I'd been taught by my mother as a child. When I looked into his deep brown eyes, I knew I'd find the faintest hint of power there, held back. This man was a warlock. Through and through.

Male witches—warlocks—were rarer than female ones for reasons no one fully understood. The known ratio of witches to warlocks was about ten to one. Even the ones who did have power seemed to have less than most female witches. A lot of warlocks with just a trace of talent looked for ways to improve on it, whether it was building up their physical strength, acquiring powerful items—such as wands, talismans, amulets, and the like—or simply having a witch work designs of power tattooed into his skin, turning himself into a kind of living weapon…one covered with the symbols of our magic art.

I swallowed. The results of a well-developed warlock who had worked at the craft for years were most certainly impressive. This is the closest I had ever been to one. He was inches from me, closer than I liked to stand to anyone who was a stranger.

"Elle Chambers," Rebecca said, "this is Evert Masterson. Evert works for the coven."

"Charmed, I'm sure," I quipped, but he didn't laugh. That was a bad sign.

I offered him my hand to shake. That is, I offered him the hand Rebecca didn't have a hold on. After a moment, he took it. His grip was strong, but not crushing, like he knew his own strength perfectly.

Up close, his voice was a gravelly rumble. "There are those who say that the very word warlock means *oath breaker*."

Well, that was one way to start a conversation. I wasn't about to let him scare me that easily. "Well, luckily, we're in Scotland, where the old word for warlock just means *cunning man*. It's not a slur, but a compliment."

A low laugh rumbled out of his diaphragm, sounding rusty, as if he hardly ever laughed. Evert Masterson was obviously a man completely in control of his own strength, his own power, his own masculinity, and apparently, he had a small sense of humor. Very small.

"You are an interesting woman, Elle," he said, his eyes flickering over me from head to toe appreciatively. He didn't seem remotely embarrassed about doing it, either.

"I've been told that…very recently, in fact."

His small outburst of humor receded back into a mask where everything was measured and careful. His gaze flicked over to Rebecca, and I wondered if they were sleeping together. Then I silently wrote off the speculation. There was no way that someone like Rebecca would ever sleep with a man like *him,* was there? There was a spark of something between them that was strange and unidentifiable. Even for me.

Rebecca wasn't much help with that. Her shields were still laced tight.

"Hello, Evert Masterson," I said cautiously.

"Hello, Elle Chambers." Evert's voice was deep and calm, but with a suggestion of far more somewhere beneath it. Like the ocean full of sharks, or a forest full of poison ivy sprites. "Wait a minute. Your surname is Chambers? Are you—"

"Elle is Annette Chambers' daughter," Rebecca explained.

Evert looked at her without saying anything for a moment. "You didn't tell me that part when you roped me into this."

"I didn't think she would become involved," Rebecca said.

"Actually, I suspect she was a little busy running after me to grab me," I added. "Now, are the two of you going to tell me what's going on yet? I don't appreciate being grabbed on the street and dragged into an empty house."

"Where do you appreciate being grabbed?" Evert shot back, with a smile that was anything but warm. It was that cold, calculating smile that stopped me from slapping him, because I had the good sense to have a small prickle of fear. The smile gave me pause, as did the part where he could probably have torn me in half one-handed, if he wanted. Something about that smile sent a shiver through my body and behind it came a shudder of revulsion. His chilling welcome transformed him from simply good looking to dangerously handsome. Dangerous being the operative word. This guy seemed like he would devour good little witches like me for breakfast. And then order up another for lunch.

"You'll never find out where I like to be grabbed," I assured him coolly.

He shrugged in a supple roll of muscles that seemed to contain a pretty clear *we'll see*. "Come through. Then you can explain."

"Wait just a minute. I can explain? You two are the ones with explaining to do. And some serious apologizing, too."

Evert just walked off in the direction of one of the rooms leading off the hall. Even steaming with indignation, I silently followed him and Rebecca. This room wasn't quite as bare as the rest of the house. It had a bed shoved into one corner, a couple of simple folding chairs, and a few bags of clothing

39

tucked carefully away. Somehow, this looked more like squatting than renting and the more I looked around, the more I became certain of it.

A couple of spirits flitted about the ceiling, more collections of raw emotion than anything, left over from all the years the house had been standing. I had to admit, there was something comforting about their presence. Not that they could do anything, but it still seemed better than being alone in a room with Evert and Rebecca. Of course, almost as soon as I thought that, they floated up through the ceiling and away.

Some of the contents of the room gave me a pretty good clue when it came to what Rebecca and Evert were doing there. Along the back wall, stacked according to a system that probably made sense at the time, there was enough assorted surveillance equipment to keep a small government agency happy for years. A camera pointed out of the window, along with a shotgun microphone, both hidden away behind partly closed curtains. A laptop on a small table showed video feeds obviously taken from wireless cameras dotted around the area.

"No one notices all the electricity that gear is using?" I asked.

Rebecca shrugged. "The rent is paid for a month. No one cares."

I nodded, turning my attention back to the surveillance gear. There was a floor plan of a house taped on the wall, and every camera was pointed directly at Niall Sampson's property.

"Really? You're watching Niall Sampson? Why?"

"So that Evert can do his job," Rebecca said, gesturing to one of the folding chairs.

I sat in it and immediately regretted it. I squirmed in the hard seat. "If this chair is meant to be torture, you've succeeded."

"It came with the house," Evert said, "and trust me, you don't know anything about torture."

I smiled tightly. "Which presumably means that the work you do for the coven doesn't involve dropping round knitting patterns for the older members?"

Evert gave me another of those eloquent shrugs of his. "It turns out knitting isn't my forte."

"So, what is your forte?" I asked. "Are you going to tell me?"

"Be careful what you wish for." Evert stretched, and those tattoos of his seemed to move. It was both threatening and curiously sensual.

"What is this all about?" I demanded, not wanting to back down from such a casual display of testosterone and nerve. "You two are completely interfering in my work and my life."

He huffed, "Get off your little pea, princess. This is no fairy tale thing."

I imagined *his* thing was a lot more dark and dangerous than the kinds of jobs I did, while apparently still leaving him plenty of time to spend in the gym. It was hard to avoid staring at him. The things tattooed on his skin were all looking at me, the ones that had eyes. I was more than a little creeped out.

Rebecca looked back and forth at us. A double take. A triple take. "Evert helps to solve problems for the coven."

"Oh, then he's just like me then," I said sarcastically. "Why didn't you say so? It's always nice to have something in common with my captors. What's next? A forced bank heist and indoctrination into a creepy cult?"

41

Evert smiled again. He didn't look any less dangerous when he smiled, but it was good to watch anyway. Like a tiger. "The problems I solve have generally gone beyond being nice to people. By the time they call me in, everything has unraveled to the point where I either kill something and eat it, or deal with the problem by reminding sassy little witches that they should respect the authority of their betters. Real work."

Oh, that was just so insulting. Like he was the only one who did the dangerous parts. Like I just spent my life running around spreading happiness, joy and good feeling...*damn.*

"I'm not always this nice," I insisted. I don't know why I wanted to impress him with that. "And if you think I'm scared of you, you're wrong."

Evert stood there, his expression unreadable. It was probably not often that anyone stood up to him. Certainly not a witch who was around a foot and a half shorter than him. "You ought to be. I look forward to finding out someday just how much you can push the envelope with your powers, Little Miss Witchy Business."

"Don't *mock* you? Don't *dare* me," I retorted. I had never pulled out the stops on my powers, but this warlock was itching to push me into doing just that. The trouble was, I suspected that even if I used all the power I had, it still wouldn't be much. I was an enchantress. Barely a real witch at all.

"Stop bickering, the both of you," Rebecca said in her best schoolteacher voice. It was the tone she generally saved for when I'd cut things too close on a job. "Elle, you can see that we are in the middle of something important here. We need answers, please. What were you doing in Niall Sampson's house?"

Finally, we were getting down to the reasons for them wanting to bring me here. Obviously, they were worried that I was going to get in the way of whatever they were doing with Niall's place.

"Insurance work," I explained, deciding that this had gone on long enough. If I waited for Rebecca to talk first, I'd still be there a year from now. As for Evert, I got the feeling he was enjoying the game too much. "Niall Sampson insures with one of the firms I work for. Earlier today, he had a valuable artwork stolen." I took a pointed look around the room. "That theft hasn't anything to do with either of you, has it?"

"You think I'd do something like that?" Rebecca asked. "Steal?"

As opposed to murdering, which Evert had already said he was fine with. Yet I knew Rebecca meant it. Stealing was beneath her. Actually, if it came to it, she'd probably get me to do it. Even so…

"It is an artifact of some possible magical importance. Or you could have been testing out Niall Sampson's security system. Either way, I want to know so that I can get out of the way before things get complicated. And before you get in trouble with the coven."

"My, my. It's a bit late for that," Evert said. "She didn't tell you?"

Really? This was new. Rebecca was in hot water with the coven? No wonder she was so upset.

I wondered what she had done to raise their ire. I also wondered if snatching me off the street and cutting me down to some novice grade of witch with her insults was some unknown way for her to get back in the coven's good graces.

I turned my attention back to Evert. His tattoos rippling with their own live moment on his skin—which was creepy, but fascinating—Evert moved over to look through the viewfinder of the camera aimed at Niall's place. He glanced over to Rebecca, a crease of worry between his eyebrows.

"Too late. By now, he'll surely have guessed what she is."

"Yes, but that doesn't have to be a problem," she replied.

"Rebecca, you know it won't be that simple. What if—"

"I'm not an—"

"Hey!" I said sharply, standing up from the uncomfortable folding chair and crossing my arms over my chest. I tried not to get angry, but there was something about Evert that made me want to hit him and I was close to it. I wanted to do something to him, anyway. Maybe not hit him. "I am right here, you know. In the room."

Rebecca sighed, looking at me for several seconds, measuring just how ticked off I was. Her expression was indecipherable, and she'd already warned me about using my magic on her. "That's the problem. Now that I think about it, this is just about the worst place for you to be right now, Elle. Could I persuade you to just let this one drop?"

"You want me to walk away from the case? Just like that?" I did my best not to sound too hurt by that. Even so, I shook my head. "No. No way. You haven't told me a thing, and I have my professional reputation to consider, Rebecca. I don't get work from the big names because I walk away with the job half done. And there is the matter of my fee."

"Even so—"

"It wouldn't work," Evert said, interrupting. "She's here now. He's seen her. And she is not going to back down from a case. I wouldn't."

That felt almost like a compliment. Although exactly how much of a compliment it was to find myself compared to someone like Evert, I didn't know.

"Come on," I said. "What do you two know that I don't?"

"I'm just trying to find a way out of this…mess," Rebecca said.

I shook my head. "Listen, I don't know the details of whatever you two are working on…"

"And you aren't going to get them. Not yet." Rebecca shook her head. "Stop fishing for details, Elle."

"It is what I do. I fish. And apparently, you two have a whale on your hook and no clue what to do with it."

I let that sink in. Rebecca swallowed hard.

I kept going. "Whatever it is, Evert is right. Niall has met me now. If you're worried that seeing a witch will spook him—"

Rebecca rolled her eyes. "Must you speak like that?"

"Like what?"

"Like you were raised on a steady diet of American television."

"I might not have been raised on it, but I make no apologies for getting hooked on American television in adulthood. So I like *Bewitched*, so what?"

"There's a whole conversation full of reasons why that's a problem," Rebecca assured me. "We just don't have the time right now. Just keep away from this, Elle."

Not a request this time. An order. And still one I couldn't go along with.

"If it's just the thought of having me around your precious investigation that's the problem, do you think that problem goes away if I leave? Don't you think the insurers will send someone else? There is a lot of money at stake if the insurance company has to pay out that claim. And if they find out that you and Tattoo Man here are interfering—"

"Hey!" Evert protested.

I ignored him. "Listen to me, Rebecca. If the insurers found out that you were interfering with my investigation and they had to pay the claim as a result of my not recovering the stolen artwork, then you know they'd never talk to you again. Or me. You think that would make your job easier?"

Rebecca drew in her breath. She had to know I was right. Not only were her referrals for services through the coven her livelihood, but without information from insurers, it would be much harder for her to keep track of what was happening in the region. Whether it was selkies sinking ships or nereids causing flood damage, it was amazing how often supernatural events produced insurance claims.

I knew I had her then. "Let me continue the investigation. I spend half my time trying to keep the coven's business private. You know I'm discreet. At least, this way, you know you've got a friendly face in the game. I have solved just about every case I have ever had for the coven, paid for or not."

Rebecca winced at that small dig. The coven had never paid my fee for one of the jobs I had solved—it was considered uncollectible because of a connection to Saudi royalty.

The two of them looked at one another uncomfortably, and it was obvious that there was some kind of unspoken decision being made. Finally, Evert nodded.

"This could be dangerous, Elle," Rebecca said. "More dangerous than you could ever imagine."

I shrugged. "I can take care of myself. I'll do anything you need me to do."

"Now there's an opening that's hard to ignore," Evert murmured.

Rebecca glared at him. There was something in that look that was almost…jealous. That certainly fit with what I could feel coming off her. I guess I was right about them before. Or, if they weren't an item, then Rebecca certainly wanted that to change. I wanted to say that I couldn't see the attraction, but that would have been a lie.

"Right now, you don't do anything to arouse suspicion, Elle," Rebecca said, snapping me back from that thought.

"Suspicion? Of what?"

"You just continue with your investigation and keep us updated. Come on. Let's get you out of here."

It was somewhere between a friendly goodbye and a dismissal. Either way, I took the opportunity gratefully, heading back out through the empty house with Rebecca in tow. It seemed like a good moment to ask her the obvious question.

"So, Rebecca," I said when we got to the door, "are you and Evert…"

"No," Rebecca said, with a look that shut me down cold. "I wasn't the one flirting with him, anyway."

"I was not flirting with him," I insisted. "He's attractive, sure, but he's creepy. Not my type. Are you sure that there's nothing—"

"Leave it, Elle. Just…leave it."

I put a hand on her shoulder and massaged it gently. Rebecca was so tense that she actually flinched. I pulled my hand away as if burned.

"Believe me, Rebecca. I am not interested in Evert. He's not my type. Just being around him makes me feel…dirty. And I don't identify with that feeling often enough to know whether I even like it or not. I'm kind of a good witch, if you get my drift."

She flinched again. "I was like you once," Rebecca said. "A good little witch. Saving the underdog. Spreading daisies in my wake. Waiting to fall in love." She left it there.

I didn't. "It's obvious that there's something bothering you, Rebecca. Something beyond what you said in there. I just want to help."

Rebecca smiled tightly. "I know. I can't explain it all. All I can say is that you should try spending a couple of days stuck in the same place as Evert."

I suspected that would depend a little on the circumstances. A nice hotel, for example, with him spread out on the bed…no, I had to get a grip. I suspected the only way I would ever be alone in a hotel room with Evert was with him as my captor. I had always loathed those romance novels where the heroine is kidnapped and falls in love with her annoying, domineering captor. In my mind, that made the heroine TSTL or *too stupid to live*. Books like that…well, I usually ended up throwing them across the room. Did I want to be stuck in a hotel room with Evert as my captor? No, I did not.

"You still haven't told me the problem with Niall Sampson," I pointed out, determined to give it one last try. "He's…nice. And he bakes."

"Bakes?" Rebecca shook her head like she didn't want to get into that. "Just do what we asked, okay? Keep us updated on anything you find out. That's your part of this. Leave the rest to me and Evert, okay?"

I sighed. "I don't understand all of this drama. And I don't think I want to. This warlock isn't good for you, Rebecca."

"I told you it wasn't like that," Rebecca said, in a tone that made me get out of there before she changed her mind and dropped something really awful on me…*like a house.*

* Chapter Four *

Over the next couple of days, I set to work. This mostly meant paperwork. Despite Rebecca's insistence that I should be careful, the truth was that ninety percent of my job didn't involve any kind of risk at all, except possibly the risk of dying from terminal boredom as I waded through printouts of sales of art, specifications for the security systems found in Niall Sampson's home, and copies of the police statements taken from his staff. Most of the time, thoroughness was what got results in investigations like this, not running around having adventures. Besides, it was one part of my job that meant I was never going to go beyond the boundaries my instructors in magic had taught me.

"Don't let yourself get too emotional, Elle. An enchantress must be in control of herself at all times."

"Steer clear of strong sources of emotion. Remember that safety comes first."

"Plan ahead. Your gift can be useful, but it can also be a curse."

The words came back to me easily, even after all this time. Maybe it was just the number of times they'd said them, or maybe it was just the inevitable mental wandering that came with wading through so much paperwork at a stretch. Okay, maybe I needed a couple of small adventures.

I got out my cell phone and texted Siobhan. Two minutes later, I was on my way to meet her in the middle of Holyrood Park. The park was always one of my favorite spots in the city, a scheduled ancient monument where I could practically feel the history pouring off the Iron Age hill fort at its heart. I forced myself to walk past it, heading up to one of the vantage points that offered a view out over the city. From there, I could see the modern surfaces of the Scottish Parliament, the stone edifice of the castle…even the crowds of tourists flocking along the old cobbles of the main streets.

My contact was waiting for me, wearing a hooded top with the hood pulled up over her face. Goblins, even part goblins, didn't like daylight much. There was another hooded figure not far away, hunched over against the sun.

"Siobhan," I said, "I thought we agreed that just the two of us would meet."

She pulled back her hood, risking the evening light and revealing an eighteen-year-old face that wasn't what most people would have expected. People often assumed goblins were going to be short and green, when in fact, the term just meant any of the lesser fey who were generally inimical to humans. Or simply stole from them, in Siobhan's case, dipping nimble fingers into pockets where she could.

Siobhan wasn't ugly. She just looked…different. Her eyes didn't match—one was a deep green, the other was a silvery blue. Her hair was bone-white, and her otherwise quite pretty features were marked by small patches of scales like a lizard's. To most people, they might have seemed like some kind of skin disease, but in the evening light, they shone in iridescent colors.

"Dougie wanted to come with me," she said. "I didn't want to ditch him when he wanted to come to the surface with me. He doesn't get out much."

I grinned. "Except for your little adventures."

Which probably mostly consisted of relieving tourists of their valuables. Honestly though, if that was the worst Siobhan ever did, she was still a long way ahead of most goblins.

"I can't just bear sitting around watching the underside of grass growing. It's boring down in the volcano."

Sometimes, it was hard to remember that Edinburgh sat on a dead volcano. It was harder still to think about some of the creatures that had found ways to live down there.

"What do you want?" Siobhan asked. "You said it was important."

"Information on a stolen art piece."

"And the money?"

I had that ready, and handed her a small envelope of cash. She snatched it from my fingers and weighed it in her hands. "More than last time. Thanks!"

"What do you spend all that on?" I asked. Because there probably wasn't a lot to buy down in the dark.

Siobhan shrugged. "Bottles of sunblock. It adds up. What's the background on the stolen art?"

"An M.C. Escher woodcut block of the letter A. It was taken from a house not far from here." Actually, I stopped at that. Had I deliberately picked a meeting place so close?

"It's a carving of the letter A? Just that? For real?"

"Yeah. It's a pretty elaborate carving, though. If you hear anything, I might be willing to buy it back. Failing that, I'll pay for information. Do you know anything, Siobhan?"

She shook her head. "No, that sounds pretty specialized, too."

"You're sure you don't know anything?"

"She said it, didn't she?" The other goblin was male, and under his hood I could see he probably wasn't much older than her. Boyfriend? Brother? Did it matter? He started forward, putting a hand on my shoulder. "Maybe we should just see how much more cash you've got on you. Give me your cell phone."

"Siobhan," I said. "Call off your sidekick."

"It's not her you have to worry about. It's me." He pulled back a hand, as if he was going to hit me.

As the hand closed into a fist that came fast toward my face, I instinctively lashed out, taking the sudden fear I felt in that moment and shoving it back into him. It wasn't something I liked to do, it certainly wasn't something my tutors would have approved of, but I knew it would work better on this jerk than any good feelings might have.

Dougie cried out in surprise and cringed just long enough for me to bring my knee up sharply into his groin and then sweep his feet out from under him. As he started to crumble, I twisted his arm, taking it almost, almost to the point of breaking before letting go. Without the element of surprise, I could never have done it all, but surprise is nine-tenths of self-defense. The other tenth is persuading the other person they don't want to keep fighting.

Another burst of fear shoved into the prone goblin did that.

"Don't hurt me anymore!" Dougie said, sniveling.

"You shouldn't have brought him here with you, Siobhan," I said. "If you can't control your pets, they belong on a leash."

She shook her head, looking almost as frightened as he did. And sorrowful. "I didn't know he was going to try to mug you. I'm so sorry. Are you…are you going to take your money back?"

"No," I said. "I still need the information. And you didn't do anything wrong. But, if you want my advice, you'd be better off ditching this one, Siobhan. There's a coven hunter in town and he would love to have a goblin boy for an appetizer. If you're with him…"

She drew in her breath sharply and I knew that she'd got the message. I didn't mention that Evert was busy with other things. It would have spoiled the effect.

She gave Dougie a halfhearted kick. "I told you she was my friend, Dougie! She's always been nice to me. Always!"

Dougie jumped up and started walking away. She looked longingly after him, with regret and shame, too.

"Leave him, Siobhan," I said again. "Even if this hunter doesn't come for him, another will. Attacking people in broad daylight?"

"He's…I…"

I sighed, because I could feel the complex mess of feelings coming off the goblin girl, and I wasn't in the mood to deal with them. "Do what you want, Siobhan."

I left it at that, heading back through the park before Dougie decided to get over his fear. I walked away quickly, trying not to run. I could feel the aftermath of even a short fight like that coming down on me as I walked back, the natural climb down of adrenaline soon replaced by all the emotions that came in the wake of its passing. All the what-ifs. What if things had gone differently? What if Siobhan's boyfriend had brought a weapon?

I needed to get a grip. I'd already slipped enough, shoving fear emotions into Dougie. I controlled my emotions. They didn't control me. And just to prove it, I wouldn't be slinking back home to feel sorry for myself and eat ice cream out of the carton. I had a job to do, and since I was practically at Niall's house, I might as well do it.

Kelly the housekeeper let me in. Apparently, she'd had orders to do just that, and to help me in any way she could. This turned out to be through the medium of coffee, mostly, while I stared at the blank space where the Escher woodcut block had been, paced the length of the room and checked the security arrangements, making mental notes as I went.

"Have you worked for Mr. Sampson very long?" I asked her.

"About a year now. He's a very good employer."

Well, she wasn't about to say anything else, was she? In any case, what did I want her to say? The answer to that was obvious. I wanted some kind of clue as to what Rebecca and Evert were doing out there. It wasn't the only reason I was there, I did want to find out how someone could have broken in, but it was a part of it.

I tried asking the housekeeper about Niall and his work, pushing her gently to try to get her to open up. Even with a little brush of power though, there was only so much she seemed to know. Her job was to keep house—cook, clean and organize household things—and that was it. I asked if there had been anyone who had shown an interest in that particular piece of work, or if he had any business rivals who might want to do something like this. Both times, the answer was no. Then she said that she had to get on with preparing dinner if that was okay, although she did ask if I wanted anything.

"I should get started then. He will be here soon. Although I imagine it will go to waste."

I didn't know what she meant by that, but it didn't matter. I had more measurements to take, more angles to check, more scenarios to imagine. If I could just work out how the crime had been committed, the "who" might get a lot easier.

I could feel the change in the house when Niall walked in. I hadn't heard him return, but there was something about the atmosphere that was just different. Better, safer somehow. The house felt right once he was in it. Plus, of course, there was the emotional backwash of his presence.

"Hello, there," he said with pleased surprise in his eyes that I was there. "I trust that Kelly has been looking after you?"

"Yes. She's wonderful. She and I had a chat about the case and then she had to go and start dinner."

It was hard to take my eyes off him now that he was in the room. That classic face, those blue eyes and golden hair. I was unable to stop staring and he knew it, I was sure. He didn't seem to mind though.

Focus, I told myself.

"I was trying to establish how the thief or thieves might have broken in and had asked Kelly for some ideas. She came up blank, though. She knows almost nothing about your security."

"That's because it is not her job to know. Only to keep things locked up and unlock them the way she has been instructed. She makes a wonderful Beef Wellington, however."

I smiled.

Niall looked thoughtful. "Will that help to catch them? To know how they might have gotten in past our security protocols?"

"It might," I said. In particular, it might help with one possibility. The possibility of an inside job, but I couldn't tell him I thought that. Not until I was certain. "Tell me, Niall, how much do you trust your staff?"

"Implicitly." There was no hesitation before the reply. Just certainty. "Why? Do you have anything that might link one of them to the crime?"

I shook my head. "No, but it's important not to rule out any possibility until there is a reason to."

"And if I were to assure you that I know none of them would steal from me?"

I smiled. "I'd like to think that they wouldn't, but there is often more to people than there seems to be. Something you know, I think."

"Oh?" Niall raised one perfect eyebrow.

"With your art collection." I looked around. I'd seen the theme the first time I was here, but it was only after spending some time in the room that it was obvious how deep it went. "Is there *anything* in here without a hidden meaning or a secret picture within a picture?"

Niall spread his hands. "It is a theme I enjoy. The duality of things hidden, but put on display. It is intriguing for me to have every piece of art I own speak of some secret, some longing, or some hidden emotion. The truth is that, for those able to see, like you and me, there are no secrets, Elle."

I could have left it there. Perhaps I should have left it there, but I could feel the sense of challenge coming off Niall Sampson in that moment. If I didn't say anything, then I would have failed some kind of test. It was a test I didn't know the rules for, only that it was a test, and that somehow, it mattered to me. Why did it matter to me? Rebecca and Evert wouldn't be watching him without a reason, so why did I care what he thought? Even so…I most certainly cared what he thought.

"You know what I am, don't you?" I asked, going for broke.

This time, Niall did pause. "Probably better than you do. But you're asking if I know about the coven. About witches and what they can do. Yes, I know, Elle. I know everything they can do. I'm what you would call a warlock, I believe."

I felt it then. The faintest brush of another set of powers. One that felt so strange for a moment, until I realized that it was almost identical to my own.

"Wait a minute. You...you're an enchanter? How did I miss that?"

"That's the word they use?" Niall stood there, letting that hang in the air. "I am what I am, Elle. Just me. Always just me."

What did that mean? If Niall didn't know the fine details of how the coven ran, did that mean he'd never had contact with them? Or did he simply not recognize their authority? Was he not connected to the coven? That would be rare, but it certainly happened. After all, we lived in a world where the magical and inexplicable were pushed underground. The coven didn't find every witch who came into power.

Staying outside was possible, too, more so for warlocks than for witches, who were more expected to adhere to standards of the coven. The coven wasn't a monolithic entity, but we had to stay within its limits. Was that why Rebecca and Evert were watching him? Because he wasn't a part of the nebulous network that fell under the coven's control? Because he was too wild or too dangerous?

It was kind of difficult to think of Niall as wild and untamed. Nothing about him was anything less than perfect. Controlled. But that would make sense, wouldn't it, if he were like me?

"Do you have all the information you need?" Niall asked me. "For your investigation, I mean?"

"My investigation?" After what he'd just told me, it was hard even to take that in. I forced myself to get a grip, taking a deep breath. The fact that I'd found someone else like me, the only other person like me who I'd ever met, didn't change things. "Yes. I've got everything I need. For now."

"Then, why don't you let me take you to dinner?" Niall suggested.

Who was I kidding? It changed things completely. If it didn't, I would have said no there and then. I knew I shouldn't accept. It would have been deeply unprofessional at the best of times, and with Rebecca having told me to be careful, it was positively stupid.

And yet, I couldn't pass up the chance to find out more. I just couldn't. Especially not when it meant having dinner with someone as good looking as Niall. Besides, it was an opportunity to find out something that might let me help with Rebecca and Evert's investigation. Put like that, it wasn't stupid. It was practically work. Not a date at all.

"What about Kelly? She was going to make dinner."

He pulled out his phone and texted her something long and involved. In fact, his fingers were a blur and his eyes didn't even leave mine.

"I'll let her know my dinner plans changed. She's kind of used to my spontaneity."

I laughed, remembering how she'd said that the dinner would probably go to waste. She'd guessed what Niall was going to do. Obviously, she knew her employer pretty well.

"Can I at least go home and change first?" I asked. It was the wrong thing to say. I knew that as soon as I said it. Why should I want to change to go to dinner with this man? It wasn't a date. "No, on second thought, let's just go."

Niall smiled. "You're spontaneous, too."

"I guess I am." Did he have any idea of what I was feeling right then? Actually though, if he was what he said he was, then he might know exactly what I was feeling—anticipation, nervousness, and pleasure—and that was the strangest feeling of all.

"Shall we?" he said, and I knew what he meant, but still, a blush went through me as he gently brushed my bangs out of my eyes and turned toward the door that led to his garage. He handed me the keys to his Aston Martin DB5.

He looked over at me, a slight quirk of a smile touching his lips. "Would you like to drive?"

✳ Chapter Five ✳

It wasn't just the exhilaration of driving his silver Aston Martin DB5 convertible that went very fast and cost more than most people's homes, but that Niall trusted me to do so. "Trixie" took the turns like a race car and I tried not to speed, which was tough.

"Is this the same model car from the James Bond movie, *Goldfinger*?" I asked, keeping my eyes on the road.

"Yes."

"But I thought they only made two of these cars for the movie."

"Are you some sort of a car aficionado?"

"I am a *movie* car aficionado."

"You're an interesting woman, Elle," he said.

I smiled. "I trust that 007's gadgets were removed from the car?"

Niall laughed. "The movie studio smoke and mirrors are long gone. However, Trixie has a few tricks up her sleeve. Hence the nickname. No weaponry, though."

"Good to know. Thanks for trusting me to drive your Trixie."

"You look good in the driver's seat, Elle."

That meant a lot to me, and I think he knew just how much. By the time we got to the restaurant, I felt like I had completely bonded with "Trixie." Bonding with Niall was going pretty well, too.

After I parked Trixie and we got out, I handed him back the keys. "That was fun. I've never driven a convertible that nice before."

"Perhaps this will be an evening of many firsts."

"Perhaps," I said guardedly.

"I just love our city, don't you, Elle?" he asked, as we walked toward the restaurant he had chosen.

"Yes, Edinburgh must be the most magical city in the world," I replied. "It has everything. I mean, I do like to travel—who doesn't?—but we have the best of all possible worlds here with the waterfront, the castles, theatres, museums. And the old buildings, so lovingly cared for, like old grandmothers, right?"

"Yes. The haunted places, too."

I smiled. "I like those, too. The spirits, they know things."

"Indeed." Niall paused mid-step. "What's your favorite place, Elle?"

"Hands down? The Royal Botanic Garden. It is like time is stopped there, and in spring or summer, I feel like I am in a Renoir painting, sitting by the water and just soaking in the atmosphere."

"I know what you mean. I love that place, too. The glass houses are so inspiring to my creative side: art and music and growing things."

Anything that touched the emotions. I could believe that all too easily. "Yes."

"We should go there sometime. A picnic. A Renoir picnic."

"I'd like that," I said, suddenly shy that he was asking me out on another date when we had only started this one. And it was hard to ignore the fact that it was a date, as much as I tried to deny it to myself.

"I must have Renoir's *Picnic on the Grass*. For my collection," Niall said suddenly.

"I think that's in a museum."

"It is. I will have to ask Marie to find out which one."

"Better amp up your security before you add a Renoir to your gallery room."

He nodded. "Yes. There is that."

He took my hand as we were walking and interlaced his fingers with mine. It was such a wonderful feeling that I didn't fight it, not even in my head.

Niall's choice of restaurant seemed like the kind of place that would ordinarily require a reservation weeks in advance. Yet, we managed to just walk right in. Part of it was obviously that he had money and connections, but I got the feeling that it wasn't just that. This was the kind of place that would have found a certain cachet in turning away the rich or famous.

In the end, it came down to Niall's simple charm, at least of the magically enhanced variety, that got us in the door in a sweep of welcome.

I'd always been taught that warlocks were weaker than witches, but one burst of power from Niall had half the restaurant in the palm of his hand. Waiters rushed around moving tables, making room for us, asking if there was anything they could do to help...

"That was incredible," I said, when our appetizers arrived within minutes.

"I'm sure you could have done more," Niall replied, which was an answer that made me shake my head.

"I've never had that kind of power."

"Never had it, or never used it?" Niall let that thought hang there for a moment or two before switching the subject. "You were brought up within the coven?"

I nodded. "My mother was quite high up in it. Annette Chambers."

"Was it her who taught you to be afraid of your abilities?"

That earned him a sharp look from me.

"I don't mean to insult your mother, Elle," Niall said. "Truly, I'm sure she loved you a great deal. Just as I'm sure she was doing what she felt was best to protect you. It must have been nice, to be so protected."

Ouch.

I thought of all the tutors my mother had hired, the ones who had been so careful to explain the dangers of my magic, so that I didn't hurt myself in the ways in which so many young enchantresses did.

When children with powers are coming into their own, they naturally do crazy things to test their powers and the sad fact was that not all witch children lived through their childhood. For enchantresses though, it was worse. Every day was a battle to keep the world from overwhelming my senses, and as a child? How many enchantresses like me had perished, gone mad or worse because they didn't have the help I did? I hadn't thought until then just how much effort my mother had gone to in order to keep me safe and sane.

"Growing up, you didn't have that kind of help?" I guessed.

"I had a teacher, a long time ago, but I have been alone for a while now. I've had to work out a lot of things for myself."

"Like what you did to get the table?" I looked around at all the other diners. "You have to be careful with that kind of thing, Niall. Using so much power for something like that…don't you ever worry? About whether it's right? About whether it's safe?"

"You want to know if I have ever hurt anyone?" Niall asked. He didn't seem angry that I'd more or less just accused him of behaving unethically. "Elle, it's like any other variant of power. We can use it for good or ill. Or are you telling me that you have never used your own abilities in the course of your job?"

Of course I had. But I'd never used them just to get a table somewhere. I'd never used them for something so trivial. But how could I say that without seeming accusatory?

"What about the risks?" I asked instead.

Niall reached out and touched my hand then, just lightly, but the contact seemed strangely electric. "What risks did they tell you existed, Elle? What did they warn would happen if you went too far in exploring your powers?"

He made it sound like they were threatening a child with monsters under the bed, but I knew better than that. I'd felt the edges of it when I got into places with too much emotion. Even here, in the restaurant, I had to keep my powers locked down and my emotions shielded to avoid the rush of feelings that swirled around me in every direction.

"What did they say would happen, Elle?" Niall repeated.

"Madness." The word came out quietly. "They said I would go mad. That my power would eat me from the inside. And they were right, Niall. I've felt it. A big room, too many people…it's too much." I paused. "You must know what I mean."

"I do." This touch was gentle. Soothing. Warmth bloomed from the point of his tender contact to my extremities.

"Are you using magic on me?" I asked him.

Niall shook his head. "Even if I wanted to, I couldn't. Even the weakest of what we are can keep out the powers of others, and you...you are stronger than me, Elle, whatever you think." He lifted a glass of wine. "A toast: to us, the only people who can be truly certain of what we feel."

That was easy for him to say. Right then, I wasn't sure *what* I felt.

"To us," I echoed.

The Orkney Lobster was divine. He had ordered the same thing and we savored it together.

"Now," Niall said, "I have to ask you. Do you trust me, Elle?"

"No." That was too blunt. "I'm sorry. It's my job not to trust anyone. Then there's my training. I was taught to close myself off, for protection."

"What a shame, when you are capable of so much that you don't even know exists."

Niall left it there, talking of simpler things, my job and my life, while the next few courses came. Almost before I knew it, the chocolate coulant came, whisked before us like a religious offering. We lifted our mouthfuls at the same time, our eyes on each other. I thought I would pass out from how delicious it was.

"You like this place?" he asked, seeming to sense my train of thought.

"I love it. Thank you."

"You're worth it," he said quietly, and in that moment, I realized I could feel the chatter of the restaurant as my shields slipped slightly. Knowing what everyone else felt wasn't as worrying as what I felt, though. I liked Niall. *A lot.*

"Will you at least give me a chance to show you that some people can be trusted?" Niall stood, holding out his hand. It felt like another test, so I took it.

After they brought back his credit card, he said, "Ready?"

"Are we going somewhere?"

He smiled, still holding onto my hand. "You'll see."

He led me out of the restaurant, walking with me through the Edinburgh evening, first on the waterfront and then heading into the middle of the city, where there were people out on every side, enjoying the kind of nightlife that only a city built on its tourist reputation could offer. It was only as I started to guess the direction we were taking that I began to tense up.

"Trust me, Elle," Niall said. "The night is too beautiful to leave it here and go home. I promise you, I would never do anything to hurt you."

Even so, when we reached the club, it was hard not to pull back against his hold on my hand.

"We should go back to where Trixie is parked. Aren't you worried?"

"No, I left a shield around her. A layer of fear. Anyone who gets too close will feel distinctly…uncomfortable."

"Oh, of course you did." I paused. "Niall—"

"Elle, please. I want to take you dancing."

"But we can't. Dinner was one thing, but dancing with someone whose case I am investigating…no, I can't. Niall."

That was what I said. What I *felt*…that was all about the fear worming its way up through me. The fear of what would happen if I stepped into the middle of a crowded club. The onslaught of feelings that would crush me utterly.

Niall nodded firmly. "We can." He put an arm around me, and I could feel the tight strength of him pressed up against

66

me. "You won't go mad, Elle. I promise. I won't let you. I will be right there with you every moment."

I glanced down, still trying to find an excuse. "They won't even let us in. I mean, I'm still in my work clothes."

"And even dressed like that, you will still be the most beautiful woman in the room," Niall whispered. He drew me forward gently to the door, where not only did they let us in, but they didn't even make us wait in line. Right then, it seemed impossible to resist him.

Inside, the steady thrum of the music was almost deafening. People were crushed together in a space that barely seemed big enough to hold them all, wedged between a bar and a small stage. On the stage, a DJ was pumping out track after track at a volume that made it feel like the music was pulsing right through my body.

The music and the emotions both moved through me like a psychic river. I clamped down on my talents as tightly as I could, standing there with my fists balled, closing my eyes against the multicolored flare of strobe lights, while around me I could feel fierce waves of feelings battering against the edges of my shields. Joy and exhilaration, desire and the simple need to be one with the rest of that huddled sea of flesh…I couldn't keep it out. I couldn't.

"Breathe, Elle," Niall said, standing in front of me, taking my hands, rubbing my fingers and my palms with utter gentleness. Somehow, his presence seemed like a calm spot amid the rest of it. "Breathe and let it in."

"Let it in?" There barely seemed to be enough of me to shape the words among all the chaos that was battering against me. "I can't. It will crush me. I can't."

"You can," Niall said softly, his fingers running gently across my knuckles. "I'm doing it. Do I look mad to you?"

I opened my eyes then, staring at him in something that felt close to wonder. How could he stand there so calmly in this thumping, thrumming bucket of people's emotions, not to mention ours? Why wasn't he bunched tight with tension like I was, trying to keep out the raw power of the emotions around us? Or, if he really did have his defenses down, why wasn't he on his knees, clutching at his head and going steadily insane?

"Trust me, Elle," Niall said. "Let it in. All of it. I am with you here and I shall not forsake you."

I wasn't sure what it was in his voice that I latched onto in that moment, but there was something in that vow that I knew without thinking that I could trust. Something utterly reassuring. Something that made it sound like nothing in the world could hurt me if he was at my side. Since I was standing there, my whole head feeling like a tin shack with people pounding on the walls from outside, that had to be better, didn't it?

I took a breath, then I let my defenses drop. All of them.

The first rush of emotion from the crowd almost overwhelmed me. I couldn't even pick out individual emotions in that second. There was just a wall of feeling, only it wasn't a wall, because walls couldn't have run through me, feeling like a hundred people were trying to fit into my skin all at once. For a moment, I thought I might fall, but I felt strong hands holding me up. His hands. Holding me in place and steady while more emotion poured into me. Poured in past my brain and straight into my soul with the glorious collective emotion of a crowd having fun and letting loose, going wild, sexuality and even spirituality seeming to blend into one thing as they moved to the music.

The second wave of emotion that hit me was more detailed, more fragmented. It wasn't one huge roar of feelings. It was dozens of separate sensations, all distinct, all happening at once.

I moaned with it and swayed. I could feel the disappointment of the girl standing in the corner who must been stood up by someone. I could feel the pure, simple happiness of someone who just loved the feeling of the beat running through them. I could feel the love and lust of the couples dancing too close to one another. It was still too much. I almost pulled back then. I almost slammed down my shields like shutters.

"Don't close off. It gets better, Elle," Niall murmured, and those few words were enough that I held on, just a little longer. "Open your eyes. I am with you. All the way. Trust me."

I hadn't realized that I'd closed them again until that moment. I forced my eyelids open, and clarity hit me. I gasped. The emotions were still there, pouring into me, filling me, flowing through me, but I was floating on top of them, as clear and calm as if I were sitting on a raft in the middle of the ocean. I looked around, and it was as if I was seeing every detail of the room for the first time, hearing every sound there. It felt incredible. So incredible that when my eyes returned to Niall, it just seemed so obvious that he was going to kiss me.

He did.

It was a slow kiss, with him leaning in tenderly so that his lips could move softly against mine, his hands moving to settle on my shoulders, not in rough possession, but in tenderness. His kiss didn't feel like taking. It felt like he was giving to me.

My mouth opened eagerly to him, tasting him, wanting the moment to last. Never wanting it to end. We stood there and kissed in the middle of the dance floor for what felt like an eternity before we pulled back, staring at each other in what must have been an afterglow, even without sex. There I was, breathless as I felt…a new emotion. Was it love?

"That was…" I didn't have the words. "It was incredible."

Niall smiled. "The kiss or the other part?"

Of course, he would know about the rest of it. He was the same as me.

"Both. Definitely both. I always thought…I had always been told that—"

"You were told what people thought it was best for you to hear. That it would destroy you to let in others, or even let them get too close. It won't destroy you, Elle. Not the way they said. It isn't wrong. It is simply what you are meant to be. Come back with me and I will explain everything. I'll tell you everything you want to know, and…oh, damn it. Not now."

I could see him glancing around the club, and I tried to work out what he'd seen. Before I could though, Niall placed another kiss, gentle again, on my lips.

"I have to go, Elle," he said. "Thank you for a wonderful evening."

"What? All of this and you're leaving?"

His expression matched the pain I could feel. "I have to, Elle. If I'm here when they get to us…I'm sorry."

He stepped back, and he seemed to move faster than he had a right to, slipping back into the crowd, and then disappearing in a matter of seconds.

With a cry, I tried to look around for him, tried to catch some sense of where he was going or why he'd run, and it was then that I saw them. Two figures, advancing through the crowd of clubbers toward me.

Rebecca and Evert had found me. And they both looked furious.

Chapter Six

The two of them moved through the crowd like knives. They were obviously in a huge hurry from the way they shoved through the swarm of humanity towards me, not stopping, regardless of what happened.

One guy made the mistake of turning to try to rebuke Rebecca for roughly pushing past and spilling the drink from his hand. "Hey, you! Watch where you're going."

Rebecca didn't even stop. She just lightly put one hand on his chest, hitting him with a blast of power that sent him sprawling. He landed on the floor with an "oomph" as the fall knocked the wind out of him. The girl he was with cried out in alarm, but the music swallowed her dismay. The girl helped him up and even through the rest of it, I could feel her fear and anger mixed in with the crowd. Things were getting out of control.

Would it have been that difficult for two witches to simply *walk* across a crowded club to have a word with me? Instead of using magic that openly? To everyone around, I knew it would just look like she'd physically shoved him over, but

71

even so, she must have been in a real hurry to use her magic like that.

Something witchy this way comes...

I couldn't run. I couldn't hide. But I had a sinking feeling that I should have done both. Maybe Niall had the right idea to flee when he saw them coming. I certainly wished I could. The only question was why he'd done it so quickly. What did Niall know that I didn't?

Evert reached me and looked past me for a moment before Rebecca stopped him with a simple touch on his arm. "Niall Sampson has already gone. Elle must be the priority."

"Yeah!" I said. "Apparently, he saw you two coming in here like gangbusters and wanted to avoid a showdown. And using all that power out where people could see you? I want to know what is going on with you two."

"We have to get Elle out of here," Evert said. "She's drunk."

"Um, I'm right here. And I am *not* drunk. Why are you talking about me in the third person, as if I am a child?"

"Your life is in imminent danger," Rebecca said. "You're just too drunk on emotions to see it. You may not be in control of your own actions."

"My life's in danger?" I said, looking around. It didn't *feel* like my life was in danger. In fact, the crowd seemed to be having a great time as they went back to their dancing and drinking. Even the guy who had been shoved down so unceremoniously was now laughing with his girl. The only negativity I could feel was the anger coming off Rebecca and Evert.

I shook my head. "There's nothing wrong here except that you ruined my night with Niall."

"You don't think there's anything wrong here?" Rebecca grabbed my arm and dug in with strong fingers. "Oh, there is so much wrong right now."

"Let go of me!" I was getting a distinct sense of déjà vu, only last time, Evert hadn't been there. He and Rebecca each hooked an arm under one of my armpits, lifting me bodily and more or less carrying me in the direction of the exit.

"What is this? I'm perfectly capable of walking, if I wanted to leave. Which I do not!" I yelled over the music. Even with Niall gone, I wouldn't have left on my own accord for some time. It felt too good in there with the swirl of emotions mixed in with the memories of Niall's kiss. That kiss had felt perfect.

Like the rest of the club. Even though Niall was gone, I wanted to stay in the thump of the music and the press of the people. I wanted to dance by myself and just savor the feeling of the place around me as I stood in the heart of a crowd like that for possibly the first time in my life.

"I'm not leaving," I said again, struggling to get away from them. "I'm an adult and I can stay in a club if I want. What is this? A kidnapping?"

"It's a rescue, you little fool!" Rebecca snapped.

Even so, I struggled. Rebecca didn't have the right to say where I could and couldn't go. What I could and couldn't do. If I wanted to stay in the club, in the middle of all that beautiful emotion, then I should be allowed to do it.

The bouncers moved in as we got close to the door. Apparently, they didn't like seeing random women dragged out of their club against their will either. The protection of the bouncers would have been welcome under most other circumstances, but these guys were only human, and Evert...well, even before someone started putting power onto him in the form of those tattoos, I doubted that he'd been that.

"I can take care of myself!" I protested to Evert, giving him a slightly out-of-focus look. Okay, so maybe they were right about me being a little drunk with the feelings running through me.

"Obviously, you *can't* take care of yourself," Evert replied through gritted teeth.

I could see his tattoos glowing in the strobe lights of the club as he let go of me and stepped forward to aid our hasty exit. One of the bouncers seemed to sense the threat from Evert and swung a roundhouse punch that would have knocked any other man sprawling. His body a blur, Evert dodged it easily and brought his elbow around, dropping the other man to the floor with one clubbing blow. I got the feeling that even then, Evert hadn't hit as hard as he could have. The other man was still breathing, for one thing.

"I am not a damsel in distress!" I complained to him and to Rebecca. They ignored me. Rebecca kept her grip on me, while Evert kept on, shifting his attention to the next opponent. Almost before I could blink, he was on the other man, kicking him hard enough to send him flying back into the crowd of dancers.

"Stop it!" I screamed and Rebecca dug her nails into my arm as she clung to me. She wasn't going to let go, no matter what I did.

A man in the club shouted, "Fight! Fight!" and other men took up the chant. I could taste the sudden thread of fear that charged throughout the room like electricity snaking out from the source that was…me. Fear, panic…it would have taken so little for Evert to just reach out and explain rather than fighting, but apparently, shrugging off a blow from a chair to palm smash a third bouncer was simply easier for him.

A ripple of emotion went through the crowd, and I knew that it wouldn't take much for me to get the whole crowd helping me. One little push of power, and Evert could have the whole room to fight at once. Even he couldn't handle that many opponents, could he?

Then Rebecca slapped me, snapping me out of it. "We have to get her out of here, Evert," she said. "Now, please."

The hunter nodded, and in a flash, he was back at my side. Between the two of them, they nearly carried me outside, where a car was waiting with the engine running. Even amid the other drama, I couldn't help a small thought about the price of petrol. Rebecca opened the door with her powers and jumped into the driver's seat, while Evert all but threw me into the back of the car, clambering in after me and putting his arm around my shoulders.

"What are you doing?" I demanded. "I wasn't ready to leave! My life wasn't in danger. You have a lot of explaining to do!" I pulled away from Evert's embrace, but Rebecca had already flicked her fingers to lock the doors.

"Really?" I said, indignant. "We're really going to play a kid's game of lock-unlock?" I hoped not. I knew the spell, the same as I knew so many others, but they'd never worked for me. "Evert, get your hands off me."

He didn't, of course, buckling up my seatbelt as if I were a child. Meanwhile, Rebecca took off at the kind of speed that suggested she'd had training in getaway driving. The tires laid a layer of rubber on the wet pavement as she gunned the engine and we pulled away.

"Rebecca, your powers don't scare me, but your driving does!" I cried out as the car veered around other cars and headed into the slick night with tires screeching. Then it occurred to me that I would never normally have said that. Okay, maybe they were right about me being drunk. "What's wrong with you two? Have you gone stark, raving mad?"

After a block or two, Rebecca eased back on the gas pedal enough to glare at me in the rearview mirror. Instead of apologizing to me for her scary driving or the kidnapping, she said, "I thought we told you not to do anything stupid!"

"*Me* do something stupid? I wasn't the one grabbing people out of clubs and using magic in public."

Now that I was out of the club, though, it was hard not to feel a little shaky as the emotions drained out of me. It did feel uncomfortably like a hangover. Not that something like that exactly improved my mood.

"I was having a perfectly good time with Niall until you two came on the scene and he…" Vanished. *Left me.*

"The coward," Evert said under his breath. "Couldn't even face us. And you don't call kissing him in the middle of a club full of people stupid?"

"No." I shook my head. That kiss, that kiss was so amazing that I was going to remember it forever.

Evert visibly stiffened beside me. I could sense the simmering anger under his veneer of silence, and a layer of jealousy as well, but there was more than that. He was actually turned on by what had happened. By having me trapped here, by what had happened at the club. What kind of man got turned on by the idea of a woman torn from a fight like that? Like I was some kind of spoil of war?

I was shocked, appalled. I couldn't even look at Evert right then, because I didn't know how I would react. I wasn't too worried about what he might think. What he might *do*, on the other hand…Then there was Rebecca, who fed me paying investigation work through the coven. Who was probably one of the closest things I had to a real friend. Rather than look at him, I turned my face to the dark window, watching the city lights blur through angry tears that I would *not* allow to fall.

76

"I still don't see how you could have done something like this," Rebecca said from the front seat of the car. "How you could have gone so far with Niall. Unless?"

She didn't finish that thought. It sounded ominous.

"Unless what?" I asked.

She exhaled hard, as if I should know what she was talking about.

"He's an enchanter, Rebecca," I said, trying to explain, trying to show her that there was nothing wrong. Why couldn't they see there was nothing wrong? "Like me. He told me, and he took me to the club, and he kissed me. And I liked it."

"He used you," Rebecca snapped.

"He didn't use me. I was perfectly fine until the two of you showed up!"

"Elle, you don't get it at all. He fed from you."

"Fed from me?" I didn't understand. How could Niall *feed* from me? Don't talk crazy, Rebecca."

"We're saying that your new boyfriend is a vampire," Evert said, with that same blunt tone.

"He's a what?" I turned to stare at him, and then looked from him to Rebecca and back. "That's...that's insane. Of course he's not a vampire. I mean, do they even exist? Werewolves, yes. Fey, obviously. But vampires?"

No. It didn't make sense. I'd run into all kinds of supernatural creatures in the course of my job, but never a vampire. They couldn't exist. I would have at least *heard* of them, wouldn't I? Wouldn't I?

"Vampires are real," Rebecca assured me. "Although it would be a lot better for all of us if they weren't."

Struggling for a comeback, I latched onto what seemed to be the most obvious point. "No, you're wrong. I mean, he's nothing like any vampire I've heard stories about. I've seen him during the day. He doesn't have fangs, and as for turning into a bat…"

"We call them vampires because it is a convenient term," Rebecca said patiently, "but that doesn't mean the old stories are true. Or that they're any less dangerous just because they don't fit them."

"So, what is true?" I asked, trying to work out a way that Rebecca could be lying to me, or joking with me. But she wasn't joking. She wasn't the kind of person who swooped in with comic relief in a bad situation.

"Things like him feed off emotions," Evert said.

"*Things?*" I insisted. "Did you really say *things*? Niall is not a thing. Anyway, what do you care?"

"Oh, we care," Evert said quietly. "You have no idea how much."

I could feel the truth of that bubbling up through him. Actually, the intensity of what I could feel from Evert scared me a little. Yet there was something about Evert's protective demeanor that made a lump rise to my throat. I forced myself to focus on the important point, pinching the bridge of my nose.

"Tell me about vampires," I said.

"There isn't much to say," Rebecca said. "They exist. They steal emotions. They steal and they steal, and their victims slowly weaken. Eventually, they take too much from someone, and then there's nothing left of them but a husk."

"They can just walk up to someone and kill them?" I asked, not believing it. The world would be full of people dying at their hands.

"They need a connection," Rebecca explained. "A break in the body's defenses. A wound. A kiss." She paused. "You feel something very strong for Niall, and he used that as a way to get to you."

"I don't believe it," I said.

"Most vampires cut people or bite them," Evert said, matter-of-factly. "Those are the easy ones to spot."

Rebecca nodded. "It's all just a way through. Prolonged contact, or a kiss…"

She left that to sink in. She didn't have to leave it long.

"You're really saying that's what he was doing to me?" I shook my head. "No. You're so wrong. It wasn't like that. He wouldn't have hurt me."

"Let me guess," Rebecca chimed in. "He showed you a whole different way of seeing the world. With your powers."

"Yes," I said quietly. "He gave me the feeling of the entire club running through my veins and it didn't kill me. It didn't leave me a gibbering wreck. He let me stand in a room full of strangers in a way that I never would have believed possible. So, you are *not* going to believe that he was just—"

"What do you think I'm doing here?" Evert demanded from beside me, cutting me off. "Things like him kill people. They drain them and they leave what's left for people like me to find. You think I want to see you dead on the floor of some club?"

I could feel the fierceness of the emotion behind the words, and I clamped down my shields around my abilities like a straightjacket. It didn't help. If anything, it made me feel worse, off balance and jittery. I could feel the dull throb of a headache starting around my temples and I groaned.

"I can see it's useless to try to explain what I have with Niall to the two of you," I said. "What business is it of anyone's who I kiss or how I kiss them?"

"It is the coven's business if he's using you to build up his powers, sucking you dry," Rebecca insisted from the front seat. "Our collective thrives on the powers of its members."

"So, how does that make a vampire any different than another witch who shares her power with another witch?" I demanded. Maybe my own anger had made me careless.

Rebecca's eyebrows went up and she glared at me in the rearview mirror. "Heresy will get you nowhere, Elle. Witches don't steal each other's powers. We share. We help one another to become more powerful and we use our collective power to protect each other. Vampires just take."

I twisted my hands in my lap, a childhood measure of comfort that still popped up now and then if I was under pressure. And I was under pressure now…pressure to admit that Niall was a vampire. I refused to believe it. Or say it.

Evert weighed in, but the words he spoke were far different from the emotions I was picking up from him. I had no doubt that if Evert and I were alone, there would be a whole different conversation going on in the car.

"After he kills you, Niall will go on to another and another and another, until the whole coven is dead." He leaned in to whisper in my ear. "There's a fine line between what love feels like and what magic feels like. You're easy pickings for a vampire like Niall."

"There's a reason we don't let them live, Elle," Rebecca continued from the front seat. She sounded almost sorry.

She was talking about killing Niall. Seriously talking about killing him.

"No," I said. "I'm not going to let you just hurt him. I…I'll…"

"Don't make threats, Elle," Rebecca said. "You're in enough trouble with the coven as it is."

"Whatever happened to the coven's tolerance directive?" I demanded. "If he is a vampire, then Niall's a supernatural creature, so wouldn't the tolerance directive apply to him?"

Rebecca and Evert looked at each other in the rearview mirror and Rebecca's face reddened in the glow of the dash panel lights of the long, black car in which we still rode to a destination unknown to me.

"Leave the directive out of this, Elle."

I shook my head. "You're the one who opened that can of worms with your coven talk. You may be higher in the coven than I am, but I know the rules, too, and I live by them, like a good little witch. But now, a life is on the line. Niall's life. I will not be silent if you intend to go through with killing him. I will not be a party to it."

Evert nodded at Rebecca. "You'd better explain the fine print of the tolerance directive to our little witch."

I leaned forward expectantly. "This had better be good because I am at the end of my patience with you two."

Rebecca didn't look like she was going to say anything for a moment, but finally, she nodded. "It's simple. Werewolves and fey, goblins and the rest if they don't do too much harm, there's no reason to get involved. As witches in a coven, we're more organized than they are, and there are more of us than of them. We're higher on the food chain, if you like that term."

"I do not," I said. "Some of my best friends are goblins."

"Goblins don't matter," Rebecca snapped back. "The *point* is that goblins don't matter. Vampires are different. If we let them live, there wouldn't be a witch left in the entire world. They're a threat."

"Are you trying to convince me or yourself?" I managed. "Next you'll be organizing a torch mob to storm his castle. Haven't witches experienced enough prejudice, without inflicting it on someone else?"

"Enough," Evert said.

"No, it is not enough," I insisted. "Are we such hypocrites that we believe we are the only supernaturals who are entitled to exist and thrive?"

"That *is* enough, Elle." Rebecca echoed Evert even as the car rolled to a halt. I looked up, barely registering that I was back outside my house. Oh, so that's where they were taking me? Home? And here I had thought I was being kidnapped.

"I'm not trying to convince you," Rebecca said. "I'm trying to warn you. Niall Sampson is dangerous. Too dangerous to be around. Especially for you."

"What? Why?"

Rebecca didn't answer for a second or two. I got the feeling she was trying to think of the best way to say it. "Because you're vulnerable, Elle. You're an enchantress and a good one. You work with emotions. He feeds off emotions. You must be the perfect food source for him. In there, in that nightclub, he had you working with the emotions of the clubbers, didn't he?"

"Just feeling them," I insisted. "I didn't do anything with them. I just absorbed the energy and I gave it back to the crowd."

"That's something," Rebecca said with a sigh, "but if he fed from you when all of that was running through you…you'd be like a battery, Elle. It might even be what he wants. He feeds you encouragement and what seems like the bloom of love and you give him back easy access to all the emotion he could want."

I swallowed hard. That didn't sound good. Even so, I couldn't quite believe it of Niall. Not yet. Not when it was the first time I'd met anyone who seemed the same as me. "He didn't feel like what you're describing," I insisted. "He felt like an enchanter."

"He was playing you," Evert said. "He got you drunk on emotion so he could do it. He is what he is. If you stay around him, you'll probably end up dead."

"But the kiss—"

"Doesn't matter," Rebecca insisted. She sighed. "Honestly, Elle, will you just for once listen without wanting to know every last thing?"

"I am an insurance investigator. It's my job."

That earned me another sigh. "You really are drunk with him, aren't you? I should never have let you stay around him. I should have told you to get out of town for the week. It's what your mother would have wanted."

"Too late for that," Evert said, looking ruefully at Rebecca, as if she had crossed some kind of line.

"Too late?" I said.

"We need her," Evert said, still talking to Rebecca.

"Oh…right," Rebecca agreed.

"Are you two ever going to tell me what's going on?" I demanded.

"It's simple," Rebecca shot back. "You're going to help us to kill Niall Sampson."

I stared at her. She wanted me to help kill him? The man who had just kissed me? The man who had shown me a whole new way to feel things in the middle of that club? The man I had just told them I wouldn't let them hurt?

"No, I can't. I won't."

"You have to," Rebecca insisted. "You know what he is now, even if you plan on sticking your head in the sand. We've told you the harm he could do, to you and to the coven. If we don't stop him, then it looks like he's coming after you and that means he has tapped into the powers of our coven and we can't allow that. The things that could happen

83

then…if there were another way, we'd take it. It isn't as though I *like* seeing you hurt like this."

"There isn't another way, Elle," Evert insisted, looking at me with that deep intensity he had. "It has to be you. He ran at the club when he saw us coming. You don't have to be the one to kill him. I just need you to get me close. Find me a way in. You should be good at that, with your job. I thought you were one of the best at what you do?"

"The best at insurance investigations," I insisted. "I'm no mastermind for an assassination, and I never will be."

"You'll do well enough," Evert insisted. "Just get me close. I'm the best at what I do, too."

Rebecca chipped in. "We need your help and you are the only one who can get this guy to stay in one place for longer than ten seconds."

"You just said he was dangerous," I pointed out.

Evert shrugged. "He's hunting you. I can't stop that. I can use it to get close to him. If I can't kill him before he gets to you, you're dead either way."

"Oh, thanks," I said. "So now, I am reduced to being the bait for an assassination attempt?"

Rebecca got out of the car and Evert unlocked the doors.

"Come on, Elle. We'll make sure it's safe inside. That he isn't in there."

She took a step or two away from the car, and I started to get out, but Evert put a hand on my arm.

"I wouldn't risk your safety," he said in that clipped way he had. "This is the best chance for you, do you understand? I would never risk you. We will be right there with you the whole time."

"Gee, that almost sounds like you care."

I was reaching for the door handle when Evert pulled me back to him. "I shouldn't care. I can't afford to. Not in my job. But..."

He bent his head and there was no escaping as Evert kissed me. I didn't fight him or pull away, despite that there was nothing gentle about Evert's kiss. There was no soft build to it, no slow, aching need of desire, and certainly, there was a shield over his emotions. They were unreadable and he meant it to be that way. Just the physical. There was just the raw breathlessness of Evert's mouth on mine. His mouth claimed mine, taking every inch of it with lips and tongue while his hands pulled me to those strong expanses of muscle. I felt his thigh firm against mine as we pressed together there on the street.

When he finally broke the kiss, I said, "Why, Evert?"

"I kissed you so that you know the difference between a real kiss and what that thing did to you," Evert replied. I could feel that he didn't believe that as a reason any more than I did, yet it didn't matter. All that mattered was that my pulse had jumped about fifty beats a minute in the last few seconds.

Rebecca opened my front door with a wave of her hand.

"Hey," I called. "I usually use my house key to get in. Is nothing sacred to you, Rebecca?"

She didn't look happy with me. "Are you coming in, or not? Evert and I need to check the house and make sure the vampire isn't inside."

"Say that a little louder. I'm sure some of my neighbors didn't hear you." I got out of the car a little unsteadily. I didn't know if that was due to being kidnapped from the club, Niall's fate hanging in the balance, or simply Evert's kiss. I guessed that it was some combination of all of it. Sometimes, it was not fun to have so much sensitivity to emotion.

"Remember," Rebecca said. "You need to find Evert a way in to get close to Niall. Something that won't have him detected. You need to do it and let us know, as soon as possible."

"And then?" I needed to hear it again, even if I didn't want to.

"And then we'll do what needs to be done. We'll kill Niall. Together."

✳ Chapter Seven ✳

I stood outside Niall's house, being careful to keep to the shadows as I approached the front door. Not just because I wanted to make sure that Evert wouldn't be able to spot me from across the street. If things went wrong, I wanted as few people as possible to have seen me. Even insurance investigators weren't allowed to go around stealing from people's houses.

What was I doing? I'd asked myself that question a dozen times already that day as I had prepared for this task. I'd asked myself, "Why am I doing this?" while pulling on the tight black sweater and dark pants that I wore to make it easier to hide in the shadows. I wore black trainers, in case I had to run. I'd asked the question while getting together the equipment I would need for the evening's efforts. I'd asked it over and over while heading here, driving most of the way with my knees shaking. I'd asked myself the question as I waited while I watched the place before leaving my car at the top of the street to walk the rest of the way.

Every time, though, the answer was the same. It was what I needed to do. There wasn't any choice. I'd tried everything else I could think of to solve this case and I still had nothing.

I didn't want to leave things like that. Part of it was simply that I had a reputation to maintain. Of course, my employer didn't want to pay the claim—a cool and overinflated £1,000,000 in Scottish notes they had let Niall declare as the value of the piece so they could collect very high premiums for insuring it. I had checked and found that Niall had paid £80,000 in insurance premiums on just this one piece of artwork. It was shocking.

It did not escape my thinking that the insurance company would like to see Niall dead as much as Evert and Rebecca right then, if only because it would save them money. I planned on solving their problem, at least, another way.

And so, I began my life as a burglar…

I'd kept away from Niall's house for a couple of days while I made up my mind and mulled over all of the ins and outs of my scheme. I'd stared at the home's security plans that had been filed with the insurers.

I'd ignored calls from Niall, and from Evert. Evert's voicemails and texts had gotten more impatient and angry.

Niall's voicemails and texts had gotten more and more plaintive and sorrowful, in a way that pulled at my heartstrings. Niall didn't want me to do something for him. He simply wanted…me.

It was obvious to me how each man felt about me. Evert was domineering and overbearing, manipulative and impatient. Niall and I clicked so well together that, under different circumstances, we'd be madly dating, and falling in love in our own time.

The one time Rebecca had gotten through—I answered only because I didn't want them to report me as a missing person—I'd told her simply that I was trying to think about it all. She'd seemed to accept it, but I knew it wouldn't last. It hadn't.

"Elle," she'd said when she phoned earlier, "are you with us on this or not?"

"I..."

"This is no time for indecision."

"That's easy for you to say. This is someone's life." And not just anyone. Someone who'd kissed me. Someone who'd given me that moment in the club.

"Sometimes we do what has to be done," Rebecca said. "You've handled plenty of violence before."

"I've *stopped* violence," I pointed out. "Killing someone is a big deal, even if he's everything you say he is."

"He is," Rebecca insisted. She stopped. "I know how difficult it is. Believe me, I *know*. I'm the one who has to call in Evert and people like him."

"Even so..."

"Elle, I wouldn't be asking for your help if we didn't need it. If you can't do it, then I need to know, and you need to get out of town so that at least you're as far away from Niall Sampson as possible. Because when we hit, we are going to hit hard, and you need to be out of the line of fire."

I swallowed, trying to think of something to say. There must be some answer to all this that would make it all go away. Nothing came to mind.

"I need more time," I said.

"I need an answer, Elle. The right answer."

"I know you do, Rebecca."

"For the good of the coven, and for you."

It all made sense. The urgency, everything. Even so, I paused. "Tomorrow. I'll come over to see you tomorrow morning. I promise."

"You'd better be here, Elle," Rebecca said. "One more delay and we will proceed without you."

She hung up on me and I cringed. My standing with the coven was looking shakier by the second. If I couldn't get answers, my career was on the line, too. And Niall's life was on the line.

I'd bought myself one night. No, I'd bought Niall one more night. He was the one who was on the verge of death here. Yet, what could I do? Break away from the coven? Ignore its orders? To my knowledge, no witch who had broken away from a coven had ever lived for more than a year. They couldn't allow defiance.

I shuddered and brought myself back to the mechanics of the task I had to undertake. I had a theory about what happened to the Escher, and whatever else came out of tonight, I wanted to test my theory.

No, I *needed* to test it. I needed something to come to a definite end here. Every time I closed my eyes, it felt like I had people pulling me in different directions. I could remember the soft perfection of Niall's kiss, the rough, demanding passion of Evert's. He and Rebecca wanted me to help them kill Niall, Niall wanted…I didn't know what he wanted, but I was in the middle, not knowing what *I* wanted. At least I could deal with the insurers' demands without ruining everything.

I needed to remember what I was. What I did for a living. Forget everything and everyone else, I was going to find that Escher woodcut block and stop this madness tonight!

I slipped over to the front door and started work with the tools I had. Manipulating emotions may have been my main skill set, but it wasn't my only one. Sometimes, when I couldn't buy back an item from a thief, or simply persuade someone to return it, it was useful to have other options.

When it came to locks, I had to take the physical options. There were witches who could make a lock spring open with a gesture. Rebecca had already shown me several times that she was one of them. I'd even studied the spell, but I was an enchantress. It wasn't a branch of magic that worked for me. Practically none of them did.

There was a kind of irony to that. The daughter of Annette Chambers was so weak that she couldn't cast a real spell. She was so fragile that she couldn't even walk into a crowded room. She was so short of options right now that she had to resort to breaking and entering.

Still, the lock clicked open easily enough after a minute or two. I knew the model of the alarm, how it worked and its weaknesses. If I'd wanted, I could probably have gotten the code, but that would have been cheating.

What would Samantha in *Bewitched* do? Samantha would have cheated and used her magic, but I didn't want to cheat. Not for this test.

I slipped inside, trying not to make too much noise. I'd waited outside for Niall's car to go past, so it didn't look likely that he was in there, but his staff still would be, and avoiding them was kind of the point.

I tiptoed lightly across the floor in the direction of the main alarm box, opening it up as quickly as I could while keeping my ears open for signs of either Niall's assistant or his housekeeper. I wasn't sure where the driver was, either— probably in his room, watching TV or asleep.

If any of the staff showed up, I could probably talk my way out of any problems. I could tell them I was following a line of investigation and testing security. I would insist it was normal procedure to see what the weaknesses were and surmise how a real thief could have gotten in. If it came down to it, I could even tell them the truth about what I was doing here. Strange that the truth would be my very last resort…

Yet despite all that, there was a frisson of danger as I started bridging connections within the alarm box, hoping that I'd correctly memorized what to do. Things *could* go wrong, and technically, what I was doing could land me in jail and make me lose my job. I wasn't sure which of those was the bigger worry.

Worse things could happen, too. If everything Rebecca and Evert had said was true, if any of it was, then getting caught could mean far more than a little trouble with the local police. If Niall really was a vampire preying on my emotions, and really *was* hunting me, then getting caught here might be the last thing I ever did. I was coming to the realization that I had serious feelings for Niall, and if he betrayed me, my heart would never be the same. That thought made me swallow hard as I made the last of the connections.

Nothing happened when I made the changes to the alarm system. That was probably a good sign, although I knew as well as anyone that there were silent ones. For all I knew, a dozen burly police officers were already on their way. I could imagine them now, swarming into the house, their booted feet thundering across the floor in pursuit of me, handcuffs at the ready. The image of handcuffs kept coming up, again and again, and a feeling of terror rose inside of me. I pushed it away. There was nothing to fear here. I had gotten away with this part of it, at least.

But as my mind snapped out of that daydream, it became obvious that someone *was* coming. I could hear the steady click of heels on a parquet floor, and I looked around for a handy corner into which to press myself. I found one and stood there, barely daring to breathe, as Niall's assistant Marie walked past. She stopped just a pace or two from me, staring at a text message on her phone. All it would take for her to find me would be one glance in the wrong direction…

I was about to send a pulse of restlessness into her to get her moving when I spotted the security access card clipped to her belt on a coiled dangling cord. Did some part of the security system require one? I wracked my brain, going through the system, trying to work out which part it was for. The doors to the gallery room. It had to be. They'd been open when I'd been there previously, so I hadn't given them much thought when I'd planned this, but it made sense to have something like that to stop access. In fact, the more I thought about it, the more sure I was that I'd seen the model number for a card reader somewhere in the insurance documents. Of all the things to ignore. *Damn.*

I shifted from the restlessness I was going to project in Marie's direction to the kind of daydreaming stupor I needed for the next part. It wasn't much, just an extension of the kind of natural calming effect I normally favored, and it certainly wouldn't hurt her, but it did make it easier to reach out and unclip the keycard from her belt.

Easier, not easy. I still had to reach out, inch by careful inch, willing my fingers not to tremble. Trying to keep the movements sure and delicate, because any sudden jerk might break through the personal assistant's reverie. Only when I was sure I had the key card in my possession did I pull my arm back and break her out of the distraction with her phone. She shook her head, looked down at her phone again, and headed off deeper into the house, texting as she went.

I waited until she was well clear before padding over to the collection gallery, stretching my senses as much as I could. Especially the more than normal senses. It wasn't like I had a magical radar working for me, but I figured if someone became suspicious, I would at least feel a spark of *some* emotion before they caught up with me physically.

It took me another couple of minutes to get to the doors of the gallery room that way. Sure enough, they had exactly the kind of card reader that would have made things difficult for me if I hadn't stolen Marie's pass right off her belt. As it was, all I had to do was swipe it through the lock and step inside, trying not to worry too much as the room's lights came on automatically.

I stopped and looked around, trying to work out the last part. A thief would have had to go in and out in a matter of minutes. More was just too much of a risk in a house where there were people moving about. They couldn't control where the staff would go. Yet, I'd been in the house at least five minutes, and I still had the defenses in the gallery room to go. I'd been a bit sloppy with the doors, but these ones I knew all about. Pressure pads and laser sensors were all wired to a separate security box in the room. And then…well, we'd get to that part afterward.

How long would it take me to crack it? I didn't know, but I suspected it wouldn't be too long, though I really had to put on my thinking cap. Even getting the box open would involve de-activating a failsafe with this model. So, I tried another way—my way—honing in my senses on the buttons, trying to feel as precisely as I could, trying to separate out the different sensations…

Even inanimate objects retain feelings or impressions, especially if they have been touched. Whoever touches an object leaves behind their psychic tracks, little bits of emotion, and intent.

Four of the buttons had stronger impressions clinging to them than the others, and unsurprisingly, I knew that Niall's fingers had pressed 1, 3, 7, and 8, but that wasn't enough to go on.

I focused more, pressing the part of me that felt emotions like a wine taster picking apart flavors, trying to force myself to distinguish the tiniest differences. Did the "3" feel like it had a tiny hint more satisfaction clinging to it? The last number then, the one that gave them what they wanted. Did the "1" have that tiny fleck of "do I really have to punch this code in again" frustration? Which just left two numbers. Indistinguishable, as far as I could tell. A fifty-fifty shot on the order. Was fifty-fifty good enough?

I punched it in and my heart skipped a beat while I waited for all hell to break loose. 1873 didn't set off any alarms, though. I sighed with relief and lifted one of the smaller sculptures at random. Off a plinth. It didn't matter which one.

"Here goes nothing," I whispered to myself as I stepped through the gallery doors.

The blare of the alarm was instant, just as I'd known it would be. Those last sensors on the works, the ones that sensed when a piece of art had been removed from the room, weren't connected into the same circuit as the plinths. They couldn't be shut down from here. It meant that they could be rearranged within the room, but not taken outside.

I'd been almost certain, but I had to check. I had to understand. I moved back into the room, setting down my looted prize and sitting with my back to the sculpture's pedestal. When Kelly and Marie both came running, I knew for sure. Mostly because of what I could feel pouring off them like smoke. I looked over at them and put on a calm demeanor.

"I think you'd better call Niall, don't you?" It didn't even take a push of magic to make them nod. They knew as well as I did that he would want to hear about this. "Since the alarm's wired through directly to a security company, you might want to call them to stop them from coming. And just in case the security company has already called the police, call them, too."

Marie, red-faced, made all three calls, right in front of me, explaining to the latter two that it had all been an accident. I sat there, looking as carefully nonthreatening as I could.

After a minute or two, Kelly actually brought me coffee with shortbread and thanked me for running the surprise alarm drill, even said it was a good idea, though she had been "alarmed."

I giggled nervously at her pun. I barely tasted the coffee, but wolfed down the shortbread in three bites. I was too caught up in waiting for Niall to show up to get too distracted with small talk with Marie and Kelly, so I gave them perfunctory answers to their questions, saying I would discuss my findings with Niall. They were quiet then. All of us knew that this situation required Niall's presence.

The two women left when he came into the gallery, without having to be instructed to do so. Niall stood there, not demanding to know why I'd broken into his home, not raising his voice, not anything. Just waiting. He looked at me patiently, almost compassionately, and yet clearly hiding something from me, too. I felt it clearly that there was a missing piece to the puzzle and that Niall held it.

I stood up straight to match his confidence, and I could feel his attention on me as if it had true weight. I felt everything that I'd felt from him at the club, plus a hint, just a hint, of expectation as he waited for the other shoe to drop. I did my best not to disappoint him.

"So, Niall," I said. "I'm only going to ask you this once. We are running out of time. What did you do with the Escher?"

✳ Chapter Eight ✳

Niall calmly walked over to the Gabriel Metsu, carefully lifted the framed canvas and set it down on a side table. Underneath the space where the larger and deeper Metsu had hung, the little framed Escher woodcut block of the letter A nestled neatly against the wall.

Extreme annoyance surged through me. Mostly at myself…that I hadn't guessed where he would have hidden it. That he had hidden the Escher woodcut block underneath a work that was all about paintings within paintings was obviously Niall's idea of a joke. I certainly wasn't laughing.

"You hid your own artwork and reported it missing to both the police and your insurers," I said. I wanted it to be clear. I wanted *something* between us to be clear. Niall hung the Escher where it belonged and then replaced the Metsu again, all without saying a word.

"Well, Niall?" I prompted.

"How did you guess?" Niall asked, turning back to me. His question wasn't resentful, and it wasn't defensive. It was merely curiosity, tinged with something that sounded like admiration. It was the kind of tone I might have expected if I had just beaten him at chess, not caught him in the middle of an insurance fraud.

"How? I investigated." I was sure the slight edge to my voice didn't escape him. "What did you think I would do?"

"You're quietly angry," he said in a smooth, gentle voice. I couldn't feel any potential for violence coming off him, the way I sometimes did when my work ended up catching people committing insurance fraud. He seemed almost amused by the whole thing.

"I think I have a good reason, don't you?"

Niall sighed. "I didn't want to bilk the insurance company. You have to believe that."

I looked straight at him. "Make me believe it."

"I would save you, if our positions were reversed."

"I know you would." And I did. Yet, I still needed to know so much about all this. Why he had done something so...*stupid*, for a start. Was it just the money? If there was one thing Niall didn't look like he needed, that was it.

"Was it so easy for you to figure out?" he asked.

"Things felt off-kilter from the start, with no one seeing anything, hearing anything, nor admitting anything. In a theft that is not an inside job, there is always something. This was too perfect. When I couldn't see how it could be done, I knew that there had to be more to it. And I knew you were hiding something."

Niall looked at me as though trying to gauge me. "You knew all along?"

I let him go on thinking that. Maybe it would finally take him down a peg. "I didn't hear anything about any big thefts through my informant, either. Nothing of Escher's appeared on the local black market."

Niall raised one perfect eyebrow. "There's an artwork fencing operation in Edinburgh?"

"*Under* Edinburgh."

"Under it? Wait a minute, your contact is a goblin?"

I laughed. "I take the coven's tolerance directive to a grand new level. She would have told me if the Escher surfaced. So…" I took a breath and let it out. "No artwork. No evidence. No way to steal it. Your staff are all too loyal to take it. It had to be you."

"And yet, you came here anyway and broke in," Niall observed.

I shrugged. "Everything I'd discovered about the security showed that no one could just walk in off the street to steal an artwork from your home. Even with a keycard for the door lock, entrance to this room does not automatically mean that a piece of artwork can be stolen. Not easily and maybe not at all. I had to prove that, though."

Niall stared at me. The intensity of that look made me squirm. There was nowhere to hide from it. Why did I suddenly feel like the one who had done something wrong?

"That isn't an answer, Elle," he said. "Why come here?"

Because I had to be sure. Because I wanted to understand. I didn't say either one though. I came here to get answers, not to give them.

"Why did you do it, Niall? Why did you go through the motions of this elaborate…*ruse*? Was it just for the money? Or because you could? Just to see if you could get away with it?"

"Do you really believe that?" Niall countered. He sounded almost amused. "You still didn't answer my question. Why break in, Elle? You could have just rung the doorbell. I would have swept you in here and told you anything you wanted. You could have confronted me about the Escher over coffee."

I shook my head. That wasn't good enough. "I had to be certain, Niall. I didn't want just the answers that you wanted to tell me. I wanted to know the truth."

Niall gestured to the room around him. "You have the truth. And so do I. You answered your own question, Elle. Why did I do this? I lied to you because I had to know all about you."

About me? This was about *me?* No, that didn't make sense. That…"Tell me everything."

Niall's eyes locked onto mine. "I needed to find a way to be around you. A way to see if you were everything I believed you were. Everything I hoped you were."

"So, you just casually committed insurance fraud?"

Niall shrugged. How could he make even that movement look so elegant?

"I would have never accepted the claim payment, of course," he said. "If it got to the point where they sent me one, I would have told them I had misplaced it in the house and found it, or some other plausible excuse. I wasn't going to steal from the insurance company. That was far from my intent."

Strangely enough, I believed him. Niall Sampson was manipulative, capable of lying, but not a thief. I knew thieves, from Siobhan, all the way up to the kind of art thieves who might steal from a collection like this. Niall wasn't one of them.

"So, you set all this up to meet me? Was any of it genuine?"

Niall cocked his head to one side. "Everything we felt was. Look, Elle, you know as well as I do that if I had just approached you in a nonprofessional setting, your coven would have told you to run from me. You might even have listened. You would have seen a warlock not joined to a coven, a pariah. If they told you to avoid me, you would have."

I perked up. There was a ring of truth in what he said. "I'm listening."

"With an investigation to finish, you had a professional reason to stay in my proximity without much interference from your coven. You weren't about to abandon the case. I guessed that from the moment I first heard about you."

Where would that have been? How long ago had he decided to do this? Had he spent time researching me before making this move?

"You made things so complicated and confusing, mixing the professional with the personal," I said.

"I know, but I needed time, Elle. Time to get to know you. Time to see if you were everything I thought you were. If my insurers had not called you in to investigate the theft, I would have had to hire you privately to recover the Escher."

"I might not have taken it," I said. Although I suspected the truth was that if Niall Sampson had shown up on my doorstep, I would have done whatever he asked. "I do take private jobs, but rarely, because I tend to get stiffed on my fee."

"Really?"

"I'm a heck of a witch, but a very bad debt collector. It's not like I have the power to turn a nonpaying client into a frog and set them on a lily pad. And they know I would never sue."

"No?"

"No." I shuddered. "And have all the details come out in public? Would *you* want the world to know what you are, Niall?"

Niall moved over to his recently "recovered" piece. "We are all more than we seem, Elle."

I laughed at that, just a little. "Yes, you told me. The whole time, you were playing me. All of this was contrived just to meet me."

Niall moved closer to me. "You say that as if you are not worth it."

I forced myself to stand there. "You tricked me."

He reached out to touch my face. "That's because the truth would have set you running, and I don't want you running from me, Elle."

I took a careful step back. Images of me running brought only one thought. "You're hunting me. I know what you are, Niall."

"Do you?" Niall didn't move to close the distance between us, but it was obvious that he wanted to. Or maybe I wanted him to. It was hard to be certain right then. "What am I, Elle? Tell me."

"Vampire." I let the word hang there, and I couldn't hold back the anger this time. He'd tricked me. He'd tricked me about the missing Escher and quite possibly about everything he'd felt for me. He'd tricked me about what he was. "You're a vampire."

"That's the word they use," Niall said, gently.

He didn't even deny it. I bit my lip, trying to work out if I should run. If I should hit him. "I thought...I thought you were like me."

Niall's expression grew serious. "I *am* like you, Elle. That's the point."

"You aren't. You're—"

"Vampire is just a word. The coven's word. One they told you to make you flee from me. But look at what I *am*, Elle." He stood there with his arms wide as though I could discover the truth of what he was just by looking. "Look at what you are. They call you an enchantress? Then I must be an enchanter. And if I am a vampire…"

"What?" I stood there as I tried to take in what he'd just said. I couldn't. How could anyone take in something like that so easily? "You're lying."

"We are alike in every way, Elle," Niall said softly. "You are an Enchantress. I am an Enchanter. You've felt it. Have you ever met another so close to what you are?"

I shook my head, feeling the tension running through me. I took a deep breath and let it out. "They said you were a vampire and that you would weave your way into my confidence. That you would try to use me."

Niall stepped close again. "What did they tell you about vampires? What did the coven tell you? That vampires manipulate emotional energy? That they can take it? Did they tell you that I draw power from others? How is that different from what you do every day?"

"Me? I don't do that."

"Don't you?"

I shook my head, not willing to believe it. Not willing to trust it. "No…I…"

"How is it different, Elle?" This time, the question cut through me.

"I don't hurt people," I shot back, thinking of everything Rebecca had said. I couldn't be that. I *wouldn't* be that. "I don't kill people."

"And you think that I do?" Niall asked. He sounded almost saddened by that, but he still reached out to put his hands on my arms. "I could kill with the power that I have. So could you. Any witch worth her salt, even a five year old, can kill. But that doesn't mean that we have to. The problem is that you don't do half of the other things you could do, either. The good things."

"I do good things!"

"You could do so much more." Niall's expression was distant for a moment, as though imagining it. "The coven taught you to be afraid of your own power. They hid your potential from you by telling you that you had no power. They taught you to hide from yourself. They made it so you don't even dare to stand in a room full of strangers with your shields down for fear of what might happen. I could hate the coven for that. Just a little. That they could claim to protect you and then hurt you like that. *Limit* you like that."

I couldn't keep from remembering us in the nightclub. Remembering the moment when he'd kissed me. Remembering all that I let in that night. Not just him, but everyone in the room. Remembering how it had felt to feel everyone there at once.

"I absorbed the emotion from you and from the people in the nightclub?" I asked.

Niall shook his head. "Not absorbed. Not then. Just felt. We rode it like a wave, and it was beautiful, wasn't it?"

I wanted to say yes. I wanted to say yes so much. "Was I..."

Niall seemed to guess the next part. "It wasn't wrong, Elle. You didn't hurt anyone. If anything, you brought them happiness. How can that be wrong?"

It was such a simple argument, but such a powerful one that I wanted to believe it. I wanted things to be that straightforward. Yet, the closest thing I had to a friend had already told me what had happened to me in that club. How much danger I had been in.

"They..." I tried to find the words for it. "They said that you got me drunk with emotion, Niall. They said you were feeding on me. That I'm nothing to you. That I'm just prey."

"Do you believe that, Elle?" Niall asked quietly.

I wasn't done, because the horror of that thought was still there in the background. "They said you will suck out my emotion until I am a dead, shriveled husk of flesh and bone. That there won't be anything left of me if I stay around you."

"Do you really believe that?" Niall repeated. "I couldn't feed on you, Elle. Even if I wanted to. Even if I *were* the kind of vampire they describe, I physically couldn't feed on you. I told you before that my powers cannot touch you, and I meant it. It is part of what makes you so special. With anyone else..."

"With anyone else, you'd be wondering about what they felt," I guessed.

Niall nodded. "It is the irony of what we are. I can see every emotion in someone, but I can never be sure. Are they happy simply because they are, or because I want them to be happy? I would like to think that it is not in my nature to be malicious. Yet, am I selfish? At times." He swept his arm over the treasures in the room. "These things are proof of that. So, how do I know that I am not arranging the world for my benefit? Yet, with you, I said it before..."

"That we were the only people who could be truly certain of what we felt." I remembered him saying it, back when I had believed he was simply another enchanter. "So, is that all it is? That you think I'm your equal?"

"My equal and more," Niall assured me. "Not to mention beautiful and clever...is it so hard to believe that I might love you?"

No. Because the same feeling was running through me. Despite what he was. Despite what he'd said I was.

"And there's *nothing* you can do that will change my feelings?" I asked.

"I didn't say *that*."

He kissed me then, so quickly that it caught me by surprise. So quickly that I barely had time to gasp, a soft whisper of what Niall was feeling for me traveled into me like oxygen, filling my lungs and giving me sweet breath that tingled through me. I had a mental image of a red rose opening to reveal sparkling dew inside. Some part of me seemed to know what it needed to do reflexively, because I drew that energy down, coiling it away in my nameless depths that I hadn't even known I had until that moment.

The truth of it hit me then. *Really* hit me. "I...I'm..."

"You are exactly what you were before, Elle," Niall assured me.

"And this was really just because I'm...a vampire?" I said.

Niall kissed me again. "I came to your life because I had heard about an enchantress whose skill and talent with emotion seemed to mirror my own. I stayed near you because that enchantress turned out to be you. Beautiful you. Inside, you are everything I hoped and dreamed you might be."

That was easy for him to say, but certainly not prove in a moment or two. Now, only a foot from him, thoughts flitted through my mind like a flock of dark birds, all flying in different directions. So many memories were instilled in me, of tutors warning me not to use my abilities carelessly, of moments when I'd shut down what I could feel to keep from hurting people. Of Rebecca warning me against Niall. Of Niall in the nightclub, letting emotions run through me...

Practically everyone I knew had lied to me about the right and wrong ways to use my powers, and the one man who tried to tell me the truth, who had risked everything to show me the truth...well, he wasn't just a warlock. He was a vampire, too. And he was the most beautiful man I had ever met.

"I don't know what I should do," I said.

"What do you *want* to do, Elle?" Niall asked patiently.

It was a question no one had ever asked me before. My mother had set out the path I was going to follow and I trod in her footsteps. The coven had assumed I was going to fall into place after her as an obedient witch and an asset to the coven. Even my employers told me what I was going to be doing with my time. Where I was going to go, what I was going to do.

"You have the right to choose your own path, Elle." Niall put his hand on my face. "But you have to say it. What do you want to do?"

Right then, there was only one thing I wanted to choose. One man. One warlock. One vampire. I kissed Niall. I kissed him with all the passion I could find, throwing my arms around his head to pull him to me. I moaned as my tongue darted into his mouth and took him more assertively than I had ever touched anyone.

He groaned in turn, his hands pulling me tight to him. When my hands moved to his shirt buttons, he didn't waste time asking me if I was sure. I guess that he, of all people, knew exactly how I felt in that moment. And I was glad he did. *So glad.*

His hands slid under my sweater, burning hot wherever they touched my skin. His mouth made its way along my jawline, kissing a spot on my neck that sent my nerve endings into overdrive.

"Let me in, Elle," he breathed against my skin. "I want all of you. Every last part."

I almost didn't realize what he meant until it occurred to me that I was shielding as habitually as I always did. The hard instinct that kept me shielding almost every waking moment of my life was still there. Still holding up that barrier. Niall's lips moved up to find mine again, before moving up to brush my ear.

"I'm here, Elle," he whispered in my ear and tugged my hair gently as he held my head in place to kiss my ears. That sensation, that small sharp pain among the pleasure, made me gasp.

"Oh!" Tingles shot through me as his lips caressed my ear lobes. Not just physical ones, but emotional ones, too. My knees would have buckled, but he held me tightly against him.

"You don't have to maintain control around me. Just. Let. Go."

The words were enough, and I felt the waves of emotions break through me. I felt washed into him, my sea of want and need crashing into his. For several seconds, I couldn't even begin to tell which of us was which. Every touch, every kiss, seemed to send so much sensation flowing through both of us that it didn't matter then.

I wanted more. "Niall."

"What do you want, Elle?" he asked softly, his lips brushing my eyelids.

"You. *All of you.*"

"Come and get it." He lowered his shields completely, more than anyone else I had ever felt in my entire life. His emotions were completely naked before me and he wrapped the tendrils of them around mine, even as his fingers moved across my skin.

When I couldn't get the buttons of Niall's shirt undone, I tore at them, pulling the fabric open to look on the hard planes of the muscles underneath. He had a dancer's body, not heavily built, but every inch of his torso defined, every movement under control as he lifted the sweater from me, then reached back to unclasp my bra with gentle but deft hands that didn't hesitate, didn't falter.

He knew what he wanted, too. He'd done this before. Niall's hands moved over the newly bared skin of my torso, every touch a torrent of sensation where I got everything Niall was feeling along with my own pleasure. When his hands went to my breasts, I moaned and arched them into his hands as they caressed me.

I knelt, pulling at his belt, stripping away those dark pants and barely wasting any time on the frustrating black boxers beneath. I wanted him then, and I wanted him in every way possible. I wanted to feel the rush of pleasure as I took Niall into my mouth and know that I was doing that to him, too. I wanted it, and I did it, reveling in teasing the hard thickness of him until he groaned above me and pushed me back.

"No, not yet, sweetest," he said, bending down to lift me to my feet.

He finished undressing me then, his clever hands seeming to find oh-so-sensitive spots every time they brushed my skin. I shuddered with pleasure under his touch. Oh, he was good at this. Oh Goddess, he was very good at it. When I was as naked as he was, Niall lifted me, seating me on top of the pedestal that had recently held a piece of modern sculpture before I'd tried to steal it.

He stepped back, staring at me. "Beautiful, Elle. I should never take you off this pedestal."

He didn't give me a chance to reply, moving forward again, his lips making their way down my body, the heat of his mouth on my neck, my breasts, my belly…

"Oh…"

I couldn't help crying out as he spread my legs wider, his mouth doing for me everything that I had just done for him and more, his tongue moving swiftly as he brought me to the edge of climax, and over it.

"Oh, yes! Yes!"

My hands gripped that beautiful halo of golden hair as I came, pulling him to me. I still wasn't done with him. He stood, and I could see he wasn't done with me either. He pushed into me, and what little self-control I had left shattered...I felt like I was floating, and that Niall was floating with me. I could feel everything around me. We were here in this room, and yet, we hovered far above the Earth, just on the edge of twilight. Every breath each of us took, every atom in the room vibrated and every molecule of star stuff spun out into little galaxies. I could feel him, the house around us, and the street. More than that, it felt like I could feel Scotland, the seas, the planet, the universe. In that moment, it felt like we were all of it.

I stared into Niall's eyes as we moved together, our bodies seeming to know each other perfectly, and in those moments everything in the universe made sense. When my pleasure burst over me a second time and he cried out above me, my scream must have carried through the city.

Afterward, we lay on the floor of the gallery, nestled together on the thick, soft carpet. I realized that the floor must have had radiant heating. Or maybe it was just the warmth from us radiating around us with swirls of well-being, comfort, and joy.

"Elle." He said my name like it was magic itself and my tears welled up but did not fall. I didn't even remember how we had gotten to the floor—perhaps he had laid me down gently. Niall was beside me, our bodies still entwined, connected by spent flesh and by emotion. He tenderly stroked a strand of hair back from my face. He didn't say anything after my name. Right then, he didn't need to. I already felt like I understood everything there was to know.

"Niall." I breathed his name into his mouth and our lips met again, this time to seal our destiny.

* Chapter Nine *

Eventually, we made it up the stairs to his bedroom, laughing, with Niall half-carrying me. We'd laughed at the thought that his staff could have spotted us at any moment. We'd ended up in his bed together, in the middle of a bedroom that looked like the rest of the house, which was to say that it looked like it had been transplanted from the middle of the nineteenth century.

I lay there with Niall beside me, just staring at him, trying to understand all the emotions swirling around inside me.

"What are you thinking?" he asked, brushing a finger over my cheek.

What *was* I thinking? How perfect he looked there, with that golden hair spilling on the pillow. How amazing the last couple of hours had been. How I couldn't believe I had actually done any of this. And yet, how glad I was that I had.

Yet, there were still things creeping in around the edges. Things I wanted to know. I tried to start with what seemed like the smallest fragment of it.

"What's so important about 1873?" I asked.

Niall smiled. "All of this—*us*—and that is what you want to know at this very moment?"

I shrugged. "I want to know everything. I'm just not sure where to start, and it feels like you didn't pick that alarm code at random."

Niall nodded, half sitting up. Since it gave me a good view of the pale, muscular lines of his torso, I wasn't about to complain. "1873 is the year I was born."

"What?" I couldn't help staring at him, and not just because of how good he looked, this time. "You're more than a hundred and forty years old? Um…you don't look your age."

It was a stupid thing to say, but I couldn't think of anything better right then.

"I sincerely hope not," Niall said, reaching out to take my hand and kiss it. His skin was soft, strong, and firm. But then, I already knew that. "This is part of why the coven calls us what it does. There are magical ways to extend a life, but normally, they take too much power, even for the strongest witches. For those of us who can draw power into ourselves from outside sources, though, that isn't such a problem."

"By 'outside sources,' do you mean people?" I tried to keep my tone neutral. I didn't succeed very well. Perhaps it wouldn't have mattered either way. Niall could feel everything I felt, after all.

Niall nodded. "We take energy from them. A kiss, close contact…it will depend on their defenses. The body holds what belongs to it. In environments with a lot of energy, it is possible to use the emotions directly, becoming a conduit for them to work with power, but to truly feed, it must be more direct. You've felt the difference, Elle."

Had I? Of course I had. I thought back to the club, with all of those emotions swirling through me. Emotions that had been beautiful and powerful, enough to get me drunk with that power, yet had seemed to fade and pass as soon as I left. Emotions that had been totally different than the moment when Niall had kissed me earlier, the energy of it swirling down into me to be locked away by some part of myself I hadn't known was there.

"And, I'll need to do that? Feed?"

"Frequently," Niall said. "Your body understands what it can do now. It will hunger for the power to do it. And you will feed your body, in order to keep you strong. You can ignore the hunger, but why would you?"

"Because it's hurting people. Because I can't just walk up to someone, force a kiss on them and steal their energy. Because it's wrong."

"It's all right, Elle," Niall said. "It isn't like that."

"Isn't it?" I had to ask the obvious question. "Have you ever killed anyone?"

His long pause that followed was enough to tell me the answer.

"Oh, Niall. You have, haven't you?"

Niall nodded. "When I was younger. I learned what I was almost by accident. I killed because I had no one to show me a better way. Believe me though, Elle, you do not have to kill in order to feed your power."

"How do you know?" I asked.

"I know."

It wasn't exactly a complete answer. I was just meant to take it on faith that I wasn't going to hurt anyone, when the coven was so afraid of creatures like Niall? Like me? I tried to push it from my mind though. Maybe I just needed time to think. Besides, there were so many other things I needed to ask.

"Before, you said something about using power taken from groups."

"To work a spell, yes."

I stared at him and swallowed. "You're talking about actual ritual spells?"

"Ah, yes, the coven's divisions. You've spent your life believing that you can't use magic. Not real magic."

"I can't," I insisted.

Niall held out his hand flat. He seemed to concentrate. Then something impossible happened. Light began to glow above his palm, soft and pale, but there. Undeniably, unmistakably there.

"But that's..." I was going to say impossible, but that would simply have sounded stupid. Like something an ordinary human might say. We both lived in a world where the impossible happened every day. When had I stopped thinking of myself as human though?

"It is not something that is efficient," Niall said. "Our skills lie in emotions. Yet power is power. If we take in enough, we can use it for anything. And you have an advantage over me there."

"An advantage?"

"You grew up the child of a powerful coven witch. I was never connected to the coven, not any coven. You will know more about magic than I ever could, even before we consider the likelihood that you will be stronger than me."

He knew a lot about me. Of course he did. He'd arranged all of this just to meet me. Which reminded me...

"What are we going to do about the insurance investigation?" I asked. "You broke the law, Niall."

"I did it for a good cause."

"Even so…"

He looked at me then. "Are you really telling me that you've never lied to insurers before, Elle? With the types of job you take on, the magical things at their hearts, I find it hard to believe that you told the truth *one hundred percent* of the time."

He had me there. I had lied. Of course I had lied. If I hadn't spent my professional life lying, then the world would have found out far more than it needed to about boggarts and goblins, the fey and the coven. Even so, I didn't like the fact that he simply assumed I would lie for him. I didn't like a lot of things, in that moment. Sleeping with him had been absolutely magical, literally, yet all of the things around Niall seemed so…complicated, right then.

I stood up, hunting for my clothes. At least we'd remembered to bring those up with us, even if they had ended up scattered across the floor like the debris from some kind of explosion. I pulled on my panties first, as he watched me, and then, feeling a blush rise to my cheeks, put on the rest of my dark burglar's clothing.

"Elle, you aren't leaving so soon, are you?" Niall asked, his eyes tracing every movement I made as I dressed. Somehow, that was as erotic as anything he had done previously. "If I have offended you, I am sorry. I never wanted to do anything to hurt you. I never *will* do anything to hurt you."

Aside from telling me that I was a creature who might potentially kill people. Aside from asking me to put aside every scrap of professionalism I'd worked so hard to build. Aside from making me feel so much for him. I had so many conflicting emotions crashing together right then. It was only made worse by the fact that I was sure he knew every one of them.

"I...I'm just going downstairs to get coffee," I assured him. "I need to think."

I added the last part *because* I knew he would be able to feel everything I was feeling right then. An hour or two ago, that had seemed like a huge bonus for a relationship, but right now, I could see that it might have its downsides, too. I would never be able to have a private feeling around him. I would never be able to truly hide anything from him.

Although he did such a good job of hiding things from me...

Niall reached out and pulled me down to kiss me. "I will be right here, Elle. Right here and thinking of you. My sweet."

I nodded and headed downstairs. I did want coffee. Things always seemed easier with enough coffee, so I set out in search of Niall's kitchen, trying not to think too hard as I went about everything I was now.

I was a vampire. I knew the word wasn't quite right, but what else was there to describe it? If I called myself an enchantress, then I was pretending that nothing had changed. I was, apparently, a creature who could drain people of their emotions, do things that I'd thought were impossible, and live forever. I was a witch. I was an enchantress. I was a vampire. And I was confused.

Oh, and I was scared because now I knew I had the power to maybe even kill people. If I wasn't careful. Even if I thought it quickly, and tried to dismiss it, that one was kind of hard to ignore. That I might accidentally kill someone. Or even do it on purpose someday. I had no way of knowing how I might act in the future. Even my certainty about who I was had been proved wrong, so why should that stay stable?

My mother had, apparently, known everything I was. That was obvious from all the tutors and their warnings. The lifetime of training me to hold back my power had been her failsafe, in order to be able to let me loose in the world. I wonder if the coven knew what I was. What must my mother have thought of me as a daughter, being something the coven habitually destroyed because it was a threat to the coven?

And now, Niall wanted me to lie for him. That seemed almost as huge as the other part. Even though he was right, even though I lied to clients all of the time, and even to the insurance company that paid my fee, that still hurt. Why? Because when I lied, I made sure things still worked out the way they should. Because even when a werewolf ran into a car, I made sure that werewolf paid for the repairs. Niall was talking like he expected me to just make it all go away. *Magically.*

That wasn't all he thought. I'd heard him, even if I hadn't quite believed him. He thought I might be more powerful than him. Certainly more resourceful, with access to the coven's magic. That made me something worth finding. Something worth controlling, maybe. I didn't know if what I felt for Niall could be real. Or if what he felt for me could be real, either. Maybe all this was just so that he could take something powerful away from the coven. Had I thought about that?

"Ms. Chambers, is everything all right?" Kelly the housekeeper was there when I took a wrong turn from the bottom of the back stairwell into some dim hallway. I'd expected she would be in bed, but no, it wasn't late enough for that, was it? It was only Niall and me who had headed there so early. I looked over at her, wondering what she must think of that.

"Everything's fine," I said. "I was just looking for the kitchen. I need coffee."

"Here," she said, reaching out for my arm as if to steady me, "let me show you the way."

That little movement to help me told me exactly how much she knew about her employer. She'd obviously helped more than one young woman in the past. It said something about how well she knew him, too. Maybe Niall had even taken Kelly upstairs…or Marie.

No! Jealousy wasn't an emotion I wanted to have, but I couldn't stop it. Niall had talked about feeding regularly like it was nothing, but it wasn't. How many women had he fed from over the years? What had he done with them? Had he taken Kelly up to his rooms? Marie the assistant? Who else?

"Come on," Kelly said. "You must be hungry."

I was, and I didn't even realize it until she said it. Just not in the way she meant. Before I even had a chance to think about it, I pushed her back against the nearest wall. Doing that was so easy, like she didn't have any weight. Or maybe it was just that I was stronger than usual.

"Oh!" she exclaimed in surprise. I could see the fear in her eyes. I could feel it. I could practically taste it. I'd never liked girls, sexually, but right then, it didn't seem to matter. All I could picture was how easy it would be to lean forward, press my lips to hers, and drain her. Every last drop of emotion pulled out in seconds as our lips touched. Or I could throw desire into her. I could make her want it…me. I could…

I shoved her away from me, hard enough that she stumbled and fell to the floor.

"What did I do?" Kelly said, truly frightened. "I don't understand."

Right then, I didn't care that she didn't understand. I didn't care that she was petrified of me. I was too busy heading in the other direction. Heading for the door. What had Niall done to me? What was I, that I could think about killing someone just like that? That I could ignore everything I thought about myself so easily? I had really just almost…

I was out of the house and into the street almost before I knew it. I looked around, trying to work out where to go. Trying to work out what to do. Home? No. I couldn't risk home. How many people would I meet on the way? People I might hurt. People I might…I couldn't even bring myself to think about that right then.

I couldn't turn around and run to Niall either, because he'd already shown that he didn't understand how much this upset me. He thought this was normal. He talked about living forever as if it was nothing. He talked about being able to cast spells as if it didn't run against everything I'd been told was possible, or good. He'd ripped away everything I thought, everything I knew, everything I was, and he treated it like it was natural. He expected me to go along with everything he had planned out, just like that.

There was only one place I could go. I knew it as certainly as I knew anything in that moment. Not that it was saying much. I staggered across the street on unsteady legs, my own body not feeling like it was mine right then. Each step seemed to have too much energy or too little, out of balance, out of control.

Despite that, I strode straight up to the door of the house from which the others were watching Niall's place and I hammered on the door with my closed fist. The spider that had spoken to me before ducked inside the broken window with a small, thin cry of alarm. It was crazy that I was behaving like this, yet I couldn't think what else to do, except ask for help, for counsel, for protection.

Rebecca opened the door, and I could see the concern on her face from the moment I pushed past her into the building.

"Elle, what's wrong? What happened to you?"

"Niall," I said. I was crying. I couldn't stop myself. If I didn't tell someone, I felt like I'd burst. No, it felt like some part of me had already burst, and I didn't know how to stop what was left from crumbing into the gap. "I…slept with him, Rebecca, and he said things, and now…I don't know what to do."

"I see. You really slept with him?"

I nodded, dumbly. "That…that part was the only one that seemed to make sense. The rest of it…" I shook my head. On the verge of tears by then, I looked at her, hoping she might have an answer. "Help me, Rebecca. Help me."

She took hold of my chin, looking into my eyes as if she was searching for something. I heard her sigh heavily. "It looks like it's already much too late for that."

I started to open my mouth to ask her what she was talking about, to demand that she just act like my friend for once. I didn't even have a chance to get the words out because a blast of force hit me at point-blank range. I flew back into the wall so hard it knocked the wind out of me and burst red stars in an arc through my field of vision. The last thing I felt was the dull throb of my head where it had cracked against the plasterboard.

* Chapter Ten *

I woke dimly, by stages. The first half-dozen times that I tried to open my eyes, pain flared in my head. As my awareness grew, I could hear Rebecca's voice in the background, and it sounded like she was talking on the phone.

"Come on, pick up. Honestly, *this* has to be one of the times he decides to go out for food? Voicemail? Oh, for…Evert, it's me. Get back here, pronto. We have a problem. A big problem. She's turned. I have her contained, but you need to get back here and do your job. Now."

Slowly, I managed to force my eyes to open. I squinted as the light hit my eyes and sent stabbing pains into my eyeballs. I was handcuffed to an iron radiator. I rattled against them, but only succeeded in hurting my wrist.

Rebecca had moved me. I was now propped against one of the walls of the room where Evert had put together his surveillance operation. My head was throbbing as if it had heard about the volcano under the city and wanted to emulate it. Oh, and Rebecca was standing in the middle of the room glaring down at me with an expression on her face that sent chills through me.

"You couldn't just do what you were told, could you, Elle?" she demanded as I managed to focus on her.

"You…you attacked me," I stammered back.

"Don't try blaming me for this." For the first time since I'd met her, she actually seemed flustered, her perfect neatness slightly out of kilter, her gestures a little too quick and stabbing. She moved like a marionette, her strings jerked in the wrong directions by some unseen puppet master.

"Why?" I asked, completely bewildered.

"Why? You might as well ask why this didn't happen a decade ago. I did everything I could to live up to what your mother wanted. Everything."

"My mother? How dare you blame her for this?" I didn't know where my mother fit into it, but if Rebecca was going to bring her up, I was going to keep it going. "You blasted me with magic, Rebecca."

It just earned me another hard look. "If you'd still been human, that would have killed you," Rebecca said. She sounded like she was trying to convince herself. She *felt* like she was trying to convince herself.

"I'm human!" I insisted.

Rebecca shook her head. She looked like it hurt her to do it, but she still did it. "You're not…you're one of them now. A *monster*."

That hurt. It hurt almost as much as the rest of it all put together. As much as everything that had changed for me. It hurt far more than my aching head. Rebecca and I hadn't been friends, exactly—we hadn't gone out shopping together or spent evenings commiserating about men while drinking wine from a box and eating bad pizza—but she'd been a kind of constant in my life, one figure who didn't change. She had always been there, whether I needed her or not. And now, I thought I knew exactly why.

"This has been your job all along, hasn't it?" I demanded. "To play my watchdog. You watched, and I guess, you reported. I thought you were there to give me jobs and support from the coven, but really, you were always there to watch me. Waiting for this. Waiting for the day it went wrong. Weren't you? *Weren't you?*"

"I was there to look after you," Rebecca said. "The way your mother wanted, the way the coven wanted. She...if it hadn't been for her, do you think you would have lived this long? You're a vampire. She knew the coven's policies, and she still tried to keep you safe. All those tutors to keep you from turning into what you are. All that work from me. I gave my life to this. All that effort and you throw it back in our faces."

I could imagine it almost perfectly. My mother learning what her little girl was and panicking, trying to keep her safe. All of the people she had hired to teach me not to use my powers just delayed my "coming out." The tutors had taught me how weak enchantresses were, that they could feel a little emotion and do small things with it, just a tiny step above normal humans. All of those people had been holding me back from coming into my own, trying to make me behave normally enough that the coven wouldn't kill me for being what I truly was. In that moment, I didn't know whether to love my mother more for protecting me or to hate her.

I swallowed down that cluster of emotions to confront Rebecca with the obvious question.

"What do you do with the ones who aren't the daughters of major coven witches?" I asked. I needed to hear Rebecca say it. "What do you do with them, Rebecca?"

She shrugged. "What do you think we do?"

"You *kill* them? What about the tolerance directive?"

Rebecca shook her head. "We told you when we warned you away from Niall Sampson. Vampires are different. Goblins, fey and the rest aren't a threat. Being generous at least lets us know what they're doing. It gives us loyalty. Not vampires though. *Never* vampires."

The sheer vehemence of that took me a little by surprise, and I couldn't help thinking of other enchantresses, elsewhere. Had they even known what they were when the hunters came for them? No wonder we were so rare.

I could feel a hint of regret about that. Just a hint, though. Most of it was anger. I took that anger and I bundled it up with my fear. Neither would do me much good now. I thought about Niall, who was just across the road. So close, and yet so far, all at the same time. He wouldn't even know that I was here, a captive.

What would he be thinking by now? That I had walked out in my fear and my anger, in some dramatic exit designed to show that I wanted nothing else to do with him? It would be no more than the truth if he thought I was running away from him. I had been. What would he think if I didn't come back, though? What if something happened to me before I could tell him that he was the most wonderful, amazing man I had ever known?

Oh, Niall, what have I done? I thought, lowering my shields and trying to get some sense of him. I had no idea just how far apart we could be and still feel each other, only that we had a connection I couldn't ignore.

"So, what happens now, Rebecca?" I asked her. She wouldn't look me in the eye as I rattled the handcuffs on the radiator. "What happens?"

"Are you still so naïve you have to ask that, Elle?" Rebecca demanded. "How many options have you given me?"

Which didn't leave me with a lot of options either. I didn't have many weapons left to me, but I wasn't helpless. I'd been in bad situations before. Not quite this dire, but if all it came down to was whether I could persuade Rebecca to let me go or not.

"You don't have to do this, Rebecca," I insisted. "I haven't hurt anybody."

I could have left it at that, but with my life at stake, I had to make certain. I reached out with my power, brushing against her shields, trying to find a scrap of the emotions I wanted to boost, to—

"Stop it!"

This time, she didn't hit me with magic. She just hit me. Right across the face. My face stung from her slap, but what stung more was the simple fact that she had done it. For so long, I had thought she was my friend.

Rebecca still looked furious, and I guessed that I'd just blown any chance I had of persuading her. "Do you think I can't feel what you're trying to do? I've tried so hard, so hard, to be a good friend. To keep them from killing you. I even spoke up after Annette died. I said I'd keep watching you. But you…you're just a manipulative little bitch. A freak. A *monster*."

I knew those fears, because they were the same ones I'd had just a little while ago, even while safe in Niall's arms. The fear that I'd someday hurt someone. The fear that I wouldn't be me anymore. I had come to Rebecca for help, advice, and maybe even compassion. Yet, it was obvious she didn't have any to give. Not to a vampire.

"I don't want to be that monster you say I am," I said. "I'm not trying to hurt anyone."

"Your kind kills indiscriminately," Rebecca snapped back. "Your kind goes around slaughtering witches and humans, and that isn't even the worst part. The worst part is that, just knowing you're around, none of us can ever trust what we feel. Or are you going to deny that, when you've just tried to manipulate me into feeling what you wanted? Are you going to deny that all your kind does is play with people?"

That was her deepest fear. I could feel it pouring from her. The fear of not being who she thought *she* was. The fear of being used. Yet hadn't the coven, hadn't Evert, done just that?

"Rebecca—"

"No. Just sit there and shut up until Evert gets here."

And what would happen then, I wanted to ask, but I didn't, both because I knew that Rebecca wasn't going to talk to me anymore, and because I already knew the answer.

So, I sat there, with my knees hugged close to my chest on the rough floor, trying not to think too hard about what was coming. Trying not to think too hard about the possibility that Rebecca might actually be right.

Was I was too dangerous to live? I'd almost attacked Niall's housekeeper, hadn't I? I'd come over here looking for Rebecca's help, but then tried to manipulate her emotions when things didn't go my way. Well, what help did I expect her to have for me? This was what I was. What I'd always been, if I believed Niall. And I did. I believed him and more than that, I believed *in* him.

Niall. My heart ached at the thought of him. At the thought of what it would be like for him when he found out that I was dead. Did he love me enough for that to hurt? I didn't know. I thought so, though he hadn't said the words. I only knew that I loved him. There, I'd said it, though only to myself.

I love you, I thought in the general direction of the house across the street, though I knew there was no chance of Niall ever hearing it. Words weren't what our kind felt. It was simpler than that. Less precise, but also purer, in a lot of ways. Would Niall feel the moment when I died?

An idea came to me in that moment. I didn't know if it would work, but I had to try. I took all my fear, all my love, everything I could find. I balled it up tight inside me, tying the emotions together with that thread of power I'd taken from Niall and swallowed down deep inside of me. I threw it out as hard as I could in the direction where I knew Niall lay, hoping that he might hear. Hoping that he might understand. Hoping that he would care if he did.

That was when Evert came back. I heard the slam of the door before I saw him, but seeing him was enough to make fear shoot through me. Before, he had looked dangerously handsome. Now, he just looked dangerous. His tattoos glowed lightly with power as he stalked forward, while his eyes on me…there was something cold about them, the anger I'd felt beneath the surface turned into something diamond-hard. His tattoos swirled around his skin in a frenzy, shifting as the power in him touched them. Oh, this was not good. Not good at all.

"He turned her?" Evert asked, looking over at Rebecca. Not talking to me.

"She as good as said it," Rebecca said. "And her eyes…"

"You're sure?"

"Of course I'm sure," Rebecca snapped back. "Do you think I would have called you if I weren't sure?"

Evert looked at her, and there was something in that look that obviously made Rebecca pause. I didn't blame her. Not for that, at least.

"Sorry," she said. "I was just hoping...I had hoped we could get through this without it coming to this."

Evert shook his head. "Hope is worthless. I learned that a long time ago."

He turned back to me, and in that moment, I knew I didn't want to die. Whatever I was, whatever I'd become, I didn't want it to end so much that I could sit there and simply let someone kill me. I'd come to Rebecca looking for help, but if this was the only brand of "help" on offer, I didn't want it. Regardless of what I became, even if there was that potential for danger I'd felt when I'd almost attacked Kelly, I didn't want this.

"It's a pity," Evert said. Just that. A whole almost-relationship's worth of emotion compressed into just three words.

"You kissed me," I tried. "I thought you liked me."

He shrugged, those tattoos of his shifting and even blinking at me. "That was then. And yes, it was a good kiss. It might have been fun going further. Now...like I said, a pity."

"I'm not going to kill anyone," I insisted. Begged. I wasn't too proud to beg. I wasn't sure if I was begging Evert or Rebecca now. I didn't know which of them was in charge. I had thought it was Rebecca, but Evert...he had the feel of someone who wouldn't be so easily reined in, even if I could somehow get Rebecca to change her mind.

"You can't say that for certain, Elle," Rebecca said. "You're not you anymore."

"I am. I'm..." I was me. The simplicity of that struck me. I was who I had always been. Niall had tried to tell me that, hadn't he? But I hadn't listened. I'd been so scared of what I might become. So scared, not just of the potential for hurting people, but also of everything I might become. The power of it, the chance to live forever, and every hint of it had seemed like one more step along a road away from the Elle Chambers I knew.

Yet, how could it be?

"You're wrong," I said. "Niall didn't turn me into a vampire."

Rebecca shook her head. "I'm not an idiot, Elle. I know what you are."

"And so do I," I said. "I'll say it again. Niall didn't turn me into a vampire. He didn't turn me into one, because I've always been one. It's who I am. Who I've always been. You, my mother, everyone else can try to deny that if they like, but it doesn't change anything."

Evert crouched in front of me, his weight rolling back on his heels. "You're right. It doesn't change anything." He reached out, one of his cavernous hands wrapping around my throat almost tenderly. "Shut your eyes, Elle. I'm good at this. I'll try to make it painless."

I didn't shut my eyes. Instead, I stared straight into the depths of Evert. I could see all of the anger there, the shell of emptiness at the core of him. How could I ever have thought that he was better than Niall? I was afraid, I couldn't be anything but afraid with his hand on my throat, but right then, the only thing I felt for him was pity.

He started to squeeze. Back in the club, I'd already seen some of the strength the tattoos gave him, but now I could feel it. Enough strength to kill. Enough strength to crush. But never the kind of strength Niall had shown me. The strength to just stand in a crowded room and be a part of it. Already, I could see darkness starting to creep in at the edges of my vision, the pressure in my head making it feel like I was going to burst if I didn't breathe.

Somewhere in the background, I heard something splinter.

Then the pressure was gone, and Evert was standing, turning from me, his hands raised to fight.

I gasped for air, and as I gasped, Niall stepped into the room, brushing fragments of door off of that elegant suit of his as if they were specks of a cobweb he'd walked through. He looked over at me then and I knew. I knew I loved him, and I knew he had heard me reach out to him with a desperate, last-ditch effort to save myself.

"Sorry I took so long," he said, ignoring the other two. "It took me a while to find my clothes."

I would have laughed if I could have done it without choking. Instead, I just had to sit and watch as Evert charged for him.

* Chapter Eleven *

Evert smashed into Niall, and for a moment, I couldn't see how Niall could possibly survive it. Evert had so much magic running through his skin that every inch of him was like a weapon now. He had so much power in him that he actually *glowed*. Yet somehow, Niall turned ahead of the charge, slipping punches and sidestepping in time to avoid a kick that burst through the plaster of the wall. Niall's answering punch brought a whoosh of air from Evert, and the two men circled one another with deadly intent.

Niall threw himself flat as a blast of power from Rebecca ripped past him and slammed into a batch of Evert's surveillance equipment, sending up a shower of sparks from the little that remained after it hit. I had been so busy watching Evert's first assault that I hadn't even seen that one coming.

Evert had clearly been waiting for it though. He rushed in, and this time, Niall barely kept him back with a kick aimed at his knee, forcing the larger man to give him enough room to spring to his feet again.

133

I jerked at the radiator that held me, wanting to help, bruising my wrists, not caring when I drew blood. I wanted to stop all this before someone got badly hurt. At least before Niall got badly hurt. Right then, I wasn't too sure how I felt about the others. Rebecca had stood by to let me die. She'd attacked me and chained me up like an animal. She'd lied to me for years. As for Evert...I could still feel where the pressure of his fingers had been on my throat, bruising it cruelly, almost snapping my windpipe. My throat was so sore that I could hardly swallow. The fact that I could still remember the feel of him kissing me only made me feel even more betrayed.

Niall was faster than I might have thought, seeming to blur as he stepped forward, throwing a flurry of strikes Evert's way. He was fast enough to dodge, too, when Evert sent an elbow scything through the space where Niall's head had been.

Evert's skin was glowing almost translucent with power now, the tattoos standing out in black light against it. Just one of those strikes would have been enough to kill any human. But we were not human, Niall and I. I didn't know what it would take to kill Niall, but I didn't want to find out, either. Not when I'd only just found him. And fallen for him...

I felt the flash of hatred from Rebecca right before she sent another blast of power Niall's way.

"Niall!" I yelled. "Duck!"

He was already moving. Of course he was. He was everything that I was. He could feel it coming just like I could. He whirled out of the way, picking up a battered camp chair and flinging it Rebecca's way with enough force that it splintered when she dodged, opening up small scratches along her cheek. She gasped and paused, putting her hand to her cheek. That bought Niall enough time to turn back just as

Evert charged him again, covering up the most vulnerable areas as the hunter battered him with blows so rapid I could barely see them.

I was more concerned with what I could feel. Hatred seemed to pour off Rebecca and Evert like morning mist off a loch, spilling out into the room and seeming to fill it bit by bit with a malevolence that chilled me to the bone. I could feel Niall pulling in their malice, using it as fuel for the fight, yet I could guess how fragile that must be. At best, he was borrowing energy in the way I had in the club. It wasn't his energy, as it would have been if he'd "fed."

Worse, he had two opponents to fight at once in a small space, two opponents who clearly weren't going to stop until both Niall and I were dead. If Niall had just been fighting Evert, I was sure Niall would have won by now. In every exchange, as fast and as strong as Evert's magic made him, Niall seemed to be able to avoid the worst of his strength with ease. If it had just been Rebecca…well, despite what she'd done to me, the thought of what Niall would be able to do to her made me more than a little uncomfortable. I'd felt her fears. I finally understood why she hated us.

Yet, it wasn't one or the other of them. Instead, Evert and Rebecca worked in concert, the way a pack of wolves might harry its prey from all sides, wearing it down. Every time Niall tried to use speed and space to move around Evert's attacks, Rebecca forced him to duck for cover with those high-energy attacks of hers. Every time Niall even thought about eliminating the threat from Rebecca, Evert took advantage of the distraction to slam home punches or brutal close-range blows from his elbows and knees.

I wrenched at the radiator yet again, trying to get free. Trying to help Niall. It seemed that whoever had installed the radiators here had done a good job, because the one I was attached to with the handcuffs didn't move an inch. It was times like this when I wished I could just wiggle my nose like Samantha in *Bewitched* and make what I wanted happen. Maybe Rebecca could have. An enchantress like me though...

Niall and Evert were close to one another now, caught up in a furious exchange of close strikes from fists, elbows, feet...anything they could find an opening for. I knew it was the wrong range for Niall to fight at, yet he had to stay close because of the threat of Rebecca's magic. He and Evert fought wildly, brutally. Each of them was simultaneously grabbing at the other's limbs in an effort to stop them from getting through. Evert shoved Niall back...

...and Rebecca hit him with a blast of magic.

Niall flew back hard enough that he actually crashed through the wall in a shower of plaster dust, and Evert plunged after him. Somewhere out of sight in the hall, I could hear the thud of flesh hitting flesh, while Rebecca moved around to the doorway, obviously looking for an opportunity to get off another shot.

I wished I could get to my lock picks. Had I even brought them out with me from Niall's house? If I had, they were tucked away in my jeans, well out of reach. I wrenched at the handcuffs yet again, uselessly, while I heard Niall make a sound of pain somewhere out of sight in the hallway. I needed my lock picks, or the spell that could open locks. Yet, I wasn't Rebecca. I couldn't just...

Except I *could*, couldn't I? Niall had told me as much. He had shown me as much with that witch light he had conjured. Whatever I wanted to do with my magic, I only had to learn to channel the power for it. It had been just one of the things that had seemed too impossible to deal with, almost as much as the danger that I might lose control. I had known all my life that I couldn't do the magic my mother had—it had always seemed like the worst disappointment, that I couldn't be a real witch like her—but Niall had told me that even that one simple certainty didn't apply to me. If he was right, and it was just a matter of channeling emotion, then I was capable of just about any sort of magic.

I really *hoped* he was right as I reached out for the anger and violence still hanging in the air, opening myself up to it, and letting it flow through me. For a moment, just like at the club, I was drowning, only this time I wasn't drowning in people's joy and excitement. I was drowning in Evert's hard-edged violence, in Rebecca's fear, in a cruel wash of deeper anger and betrayal from both of them. It was too much.

No, it couldn't be too much. I wouldn't let it be too much. Instead, I opened myself further, pulling more of it in—all of the hatred, malice, and dark intent sucked into me like a funeral dirge. It was deep and ominous and the most evil thing I had ever let myself absorb from others.

I couldn't get a solid grip on it—this wasn't power I had taken from someone—but I could ride it, and I could shape it. I'd practiced that opening spell so many times as a girl, along with so many more, hoping that *this* time one of the spells would work and I would be like my mother. I'd always lacked the raw magical power. Now though, I had all the power I needed. I just had to hold the shape of the spell. I held it and I let power flow through it like dark water through a channel, focusing the emotions around me, dragging them into the shape I needed…

The lock on the handcuffs clicked open with a crisp pop, and I was already standing, ignoring the pain in my battered head. No, not ignoring it. Healing it. My body seemed to know what it needed to do with the power rushing through it. I ran out into the hallway.

"Niall!"

Niall was somehow on his feet, still battling with Evert. He was bloodied and bruised though, his shirt ripped to show expanses of muscled flesh, his knuckles torn from the violence. And he was in trouble. *Big trouble.* Evert had managed to spin him around so that his back was to the door, which meant Rebecca had a clear shot at him. In the narrow space of the hallway, there was no way she would miss.

"Oh, no, you don't!"

I grabbed her arm, kicking her legs out from under her as I pulled her off balance, sending her arm toward the ceiling as power shot from her fingers. Ceiling plaster rained down on us in big chunks of dust and debris; even the slats behind the plaster broke and fell. She started to turn into me and I hit her open-handed, enjoying the crack of the slap as it momentarily sent her sprawling. Exactly as she had slapped me. Tit for tat.

"I'll kill you," she snarled, struggling to her knees and calling up power. With no room to dodge, I threw myself at her, plowing into her in a tangle of flailing limbs. I was stronger, and it seemed as if I knew more about fighting, but Rebecca had her magic than me and she knew how to wield it like a sword. She'd already proved that when she'd slammed me into unconsciousness before. If she even brought one spell to bear on me, it would be over, while her own defenses…

…weren't there. I looked down at the scratches along her cheek from the splinters of chair, lines of redness marring her otherwise pristine skin, ignoring the ceiling plaster and dust on her. That didn't matter. Only the scratches mattered. The damage to her wasn't much, but it was something. A way in. A break in the body's protections.

I reached out to touch Rebecca's cheek and she didn't seem to see the danger. Instead, she lifted her hand, focusing on me, the heat of her anger almost as palpable as the force of her magic. Through those tiny breaks in her flesh beneath my fingers, I reached out and pulled.

"No…"

Rebecca's spell died on her lips as I pulled the power from her and into me, down into those depths where invisible coils seemed to wrap around it, making it a part of me, devouring it. For the first time since I'd left Niall's house, I didn't feel hungry.

"You can't—" she began.

"I can. And I am!" I reached down for the fear I'd felt when Evert's hand had been around my throat. For all the times I'd been told by my tutors that I was wrong for feeling anything, for every trace of hurt I'd felt when Rebecca had attacked me, I took all of that and I shoved it into her like a weapon.

Rebecca screamed, her back arcing as if in agony. "No…please."

I kept my hold on her, pulling back what I'd pushed into her, along with a single, delicious tendril of fear that was all her own making. It was so easy to see what I could do with that. Behind me, I could hear the sounds of the men's fight continuing, but right then, I didn't care. My focus was totally on Rebecca.

"It would be so easy to kill you," I said as she cowered back. "I could push fear into you and drag it out again and again. I could leave nothing but a vegetable, destined to spend the rest of your miserable life in a straitjacket. I could use pleasure, and have you begging me for more while I killed you. I could strip away every last iota of energy from your body and leave nothing but a husk that would be taken away by the wind, like chaff in a field."

Rebecca started to build up power again, but I pulled it away from her as easily as I had done the first time.

"Every time you try to use power to retaliate against me, I can and will pull it away from you. Every time you rise up against me, you only make me stronger."

"No!" she cried out, absolutely terrified. I saw it in her eyes. I felt it crawling on her skin. I knew everything that terrified her. She was being reduced as a witch, moment by moment. The part within me that swallowed it rose up, looking for more, hungering for it again. It would have been so easy to give into that part, and then Rebecca would have died, because that part of me could have devoured the world and still been hungry.

"Don't kill me," she begged. She sounded so small then. So weak.

"I could do worse than kill you," I said, and I could. I could see all the possibilities laid out so perfectly. "I could leave you alive, but make you love me. I could twist you up so much inside that you would do anything I asked, and thank me for the opportunity. There might still be a little part of you left that knew, but it wouldn't make any difference. I could do that, Rebecca."

She dissolved into sobs. With my power, I pushed her to her knees. I could do it so easily. Kill her. I could see how. It was like I'd always known how, but was only just now remembering it. I could turn Rebecca into a shell or a puppet, make her die screaming in terror or send her to madness, all as easily as snapping my fingers. And because I knew I could, I didn't have to. I could choose.

And in that moment, I *chose*.

I leaned forward, holding Rebecca in place with an effort of my will, moving until my lips barely brushed her forehead.

She quit sobbing and raised her eyes to me in utter shock, her mascara ruined and the thick layer of chic makeup crackling off her face like the rest of her façade.

"Just be grateful that I'm not the monster you think I am," I whispered. I shoved her back onto the floor and, as she grabbed her handbag off the floor and crawled through the debris on her hands and knees, I turned back toward Niall. I heard Rebecca scramble out the front door and a few moments later, a car started.

Evert was down on the floor in a motionless heap. Just as I'd guessed, without Rebecca there to help him, he hadn't possessed enough power to overcome Niall. I didn't bother checking to see if he was still breathing. I could feel the emptiness there that signaled death.

Gingerly, I stepped over Evert's crumpled body to meet Niall's eyes. Niall looked nervous, as though worried about how I might react to the sight of him standing there over a body. I answered that question very simply, stepping closer to him and kissing him with nothing held back. In my short history of kissing Niall, it was the best to date. We ended our tender kiss slowly. I guessed that neither of us wanted to be the last to break it off.

When we eventually did, I stared at Niall. Despite everything that had just happened, he looked pristine again, although his clothes were ruined. Not that I *minded* being able to see that much of him.

"Niall, you came for me," I said. "You *heard* me."

Niall smiled. "You sound surprised. I will always come for you, Elle. If you are ever lost from me, I will always hear you, I will always feel you, and I will always follow you. I will always bring you home. *Always.*"

Always. That word, spoken multiple times—like a vow—was enough to make me swallow hard. In theory, we could have...forever. I wasn't sure if I could deal with forever just yet. On the other hand, as Niall put an arm around me and we stepped out of that demolished house together, I guessed that I could learn.

* Chapter Twelve *

I sat in the converted warehouse that made up Edinburgh's City Art Centre, admiring Niall's contribution to their collection while I waited. The Escher woodcut block of the letter A looked pretty good in its new home, even if I did say so myself. Which was just as well, because it was going to be there on loan for the foreseeable future.

I sat, looking at that simple woodcut, the letter A that meant so much to Escher, to de Mesquita, and more recently, to Niall. Would he come here, I wondered, to try to decode more of the symbols carved around the edge? Would he pass that job on to scholars? Did it even matter? When all was said and done, the woodcut had simply been a means to an end for Niall, which wasn't the way he should have treated something with that history. Escher's teacher deserved better than that.

So did I. Giving the Escher to the museum had been my price extracted from Niall for my efforts in sparing him from having to confront the insurance company about the claim. My price for having to produce a report that suggested a minor thief had been involved, who had panicked when it became obvious that G&P's crack investigator was on the case. Although I didn't put it in quite those terms. So, naturally, a couple of weeks ago, albeit with great reverence for its significance, the Escher woodcut block had been "anonymously" handed over to the museum.

It took much prompting to get Niall to confirm the gift. Sorry, the *loan*. He was quite clear about that part. Just as I was quite clear about the part where he had also generously agreed to allow the public access to some of his collection at the museum, citing the idea that there would be better security to satisfy his insurers.

The claims department was satisfied, even if they weren't entirely sure about how things had worked out that way. They had even paid me, which was one thing I wasn't expecting to get out of the situation. £100,000! The only reason I didn't return the money was because it would have looked suspicious.

Well, that and because I knew I had solved the case of the missing Escher, fair and square, even if no one else did.

It was enough money to buy me breathing space. To work out what I wanted to do with my skills and talents. Although Niall would have given me money to begin my new life, I wouldn't have taken it from him. He'd given me enough.

Niall…well, he was at least happy that I was happy, even if it meant that part of his collection had left his private gallery room and moved into a museum. He perked up a bit once I pointed out all of the empty pedestals that left in his home, and the empty wall spots, too, and how much fun we'd had with just one piece of artwork.

Eventually though, I knew that we'd need to sort things out. All of which had left me sitting in the gallery with my back to the rest of the room, waiting. Waiting and enjoying the swirl of the people around me. It was the middle of a working day, so it wasn't as busy as it could have been, yet there were still plenty of tourists around, the emotions of the crowd shifting and changing as they ran through me. It was certainly a whole new way of appreciating art.

I wasn't just there for the art though, and when I felt the emotions changing behind me, bringing back a familiar taste, I stood up.

"Hello, Rebecca," I said, turning around.

She looked different today. She was still just as carefully dressed as ever, still trying to look professional, but there was something less stern about her. Almost...*smaller*. Certainly less confident. I could feel the edge of fear radiating from her as she stood there, obviously not knowing how to start our conversation.

"You're looking good, really good," I said, trying for the gentlest smile I could. "Do you want to sit down?"

"You came alone." She sounded surprised. She actually looked around. "I thought you would bring...*him*."

"Niall. His name is Niall." I stopped. It wasn't early enough in the conversation to bring anger into it. "I said I would come alone, Rebecca. I keep my word."

I'd come to a public place, although that was as much for Rebecca's comfort as mine. She had even been the one to suggest it, though I had picked the spot. I guess she didn't want to risk meeting me in private. I didn't blame her for being cautious.

She had presumably been the one to deal with Evert's body, and even two weeks later, I could feel the fragility in her. The weakness where what I had taken from her was only just starting to heal over and regrow. I saw the first sign of a wrinkle that could not be covered by makeup, and under the concealer stick, puffiness under her eyes. She had not been sleeping well.

"Please sit down, Rebecca," I said, actually moving to sit again myself. "You're making me nervous, towering over me like that. And it was not necessary to bring a weapon, so just don't even take it out."

She sighed. "I thought you were going to—"

"No, I'm not going to make you do anything," I said with a sigh, looking up at her as I sat there. "You really think I'd do that—hurt you, don't you?"

She didn't answer, but she did sit down. Not quite next to me, she slid down in the next seat, with her defenses buttoned up tight against any possibility that I might be able to get through them. Would it do any good if I really wanted to hurt her? Thankfully, there was no reason to find out.

"You didn't run," Rebecca said, sounding surprised.

"Run?"

"Everyone in the coven thought you would run."

No, we hadn't run. Niall had suggested it almost as soon as we got back to his house, but I wasn't going to admit that to Rebecca. He had said we should get on a plane or a boat, not even stopping long enough for me to get my things. He'd said there would be more hunters like Evert coming my way, or worse. That the coven wouldn't be done with us.

"I'm not going to give up my life that easily," I said, looking across at her. "This is my life, here, and I have worked for years to build what I have. I'm not about to let what I am change it. I'm not going to spend the rest of my life on the run, just one step ahead of coven hunters. I love Edinburgh. I'm not about to leave it."

"And you think the coven will just let you keep living here?" Rebecca asked. "You think they'll leave vampires alone? Let you live so you can kill us?"

I cocked my head to one side. "I didn't kill *you*."

Rebecca froze, obviously uncomfortable. Good. Just because I didn't want to kill her, that didn't mean we were suddenly best friends. "That isn't the point."

"Really? I think it's exactly the point," I said. "I had only just learned what I was, I was as emotionally messed up as I'd ever been, I was hungry, and you had just tried to kill me." I tried to keep my tone calm when it came to that part. I wanted to show Rebecca that I was over it, that we could somehow go on in the same city without stooping to violence. I needed her to believe that part, or this whole meeting was a waste of time. "All of that, and I still didn't kill you."

"Even so—"

"You know why not, Rebecca?" I didn't wait for her answer. "Because I'm still me, and I don't kill people."

Rebecca stared at me for several seconds. "You probably think that, Elle, but how can you be sure?"

"How can I be sure?" I shrugged. "How can I know you won't turn around and start blasting people with magic? I mean, you already have experience when it comes to that kind of thing, right? So, how do I know that one of these tour groups isn't about to be blasted across the gallery?"

She at least had the grace to look embarrassed.

"So, you're asking the coven to let you live," she said, "on the basis that you haven't killed anyone yet? And I emphasize the word, 'yet.'"

I laughed. Several people in the gallery turned to look at me disapprovingly, although once they saw me, they seemed happier about it. Most of the men, at least.

"I'm not asking the coven to *let* me do anything," I said. "Do you know why the coven is so afraid of enchantresses like me, Rebecca? Have you worked out the real reason that they kill us? The reason they hate us so much?"

"Because you hurt people," Rebecca said. "Because you take them and control them. Because you hunt witches."

At least she was consistent. I guessed, after how much I'd scared her back at the house, that she had plenty of reasons to be worried. Besides, her being consistent was better somehow. It meant she'd actually believed it when she'd tried to kill me. It hadn't just been an excuse.

"No," I said. "We are not just vampires, we are very powerful witches. They hunt us because we are more powerful than them." I left that to sink in for a second or two. "Because they're worried that if they don't hunt us now, there might come a day when they aren't able to. If I wanted to, I could walk into any coven meeting, and no one would think I was weak."

"You think you're your mother?" Rebecca demanded.

I paused. "I love my mother. She protected me, but she could have done more. And no, I don't think I'm her. I'm more powerful than that."

"More powerful than your mother?" Rebecca sounded like she wanted to laugh then, but she didn't dare. "You're really mad enough to think that you're even more powerful than the coven?"

I carefully reached out, turning the attention of the crowd away from us, and I moved. Not far. Just into the next seat over, the one Rebecca hadn't wanted to occupy because it was too close.

"Yes," I said simply. "I think I am more powerful than my mother. More powerful than the coven. In fact, I know it. I have my mother's old spell books at home. I have all the spells in my head that I was never able to get working, and now I have the power to go with them."

Carefully, still keeping anyone from watching, I held out my hand. The witch light that appeared above it wasn't much, but it felt appropriate. It had been the same spell Niall had used to prove it to me, after all.

Rebecca's mouth actually fell open in shock.

"I hope your face doesn't stay like that," I said. "What? Didn't they tell you this part of what enchantresses can do?"

Just from her expression, it was obvious that the coven *hadn't* told Rebecca that part. I snuffed out the witch light in my palm.

"I have my mother's old books," I said. "I have the knowledge to work out anything I don't have from first principles. There are spells that…well, the whole coven could probably cast them, given enough time and effort. You know the kind of thing I'm talking about."

I waited, letting it sink in. Letting her think of all the possibilities. In coven circles, it was said that the eruption of Vesuvius that swallowed Pompeii was the final act in a war between two of the coven's precursors. We were sitting on top of a supposedly extinct volcano in Edinburgh and that seemed like a fact worth remembering.

"You cannot possibly become a spell caster. And there is no way that you could match the whole coven."

"Really? All I would need would be enough emotion," I said, once I'd given Rebecca a second or two. "A true witch would need a whole coven of friends, and weeks of preparations to cast a spell. Me? Well, how much emotion do you think I'd get if I went over to Glasgow and stood in the stands while Celtic played Rangers in a cup tie?"

It was a bluff, of course. I had no way of knowing what I could do, but I was pretty sure that I didn't have any easy "kill all the coven" spells hanging around or hiding up my sleeve. I would have noticed. Even if I had, did anyone really think that mass murder was on my agenda?

"You wouldn't do something like that," Rebecca said, as though she didn't feel certain.

"Well, that's the beautiful part of this, isn't it?" I smiled as I said it, trying hard to remember not to let out power to make her feel better. I didn't think she'd appreciate that.

"Either you don't believe that I would ever do something like that, in which case you're basically saying that I'm still me and there's no reason to want me dead, or you think that I might, in which case you really do not want to try anything stupid."

Rebecca pinched the bridge of her nose as if she had a terrible headache coming on.

"I can fix that tension headache for you. Unless you don't trust me."

"You…you can never just make anything easy, can you, Elle?" She looked at me as though remembering that I was the last person she wanted to offend. "That is…I…"

"It's fine," I said, standing and moving carefully back to my original seat. "I want this to be easy, Rebecca. Easy for everyone. You, me, Niall, the coven. Everyone."

"So, what do you want from the coven?" Rebecca asked. "And from me?"

Funny, Niall had asked me the same question when I refused to leave Edinburgh.

"I just want to get on with my life," I said to Rebecca with a shrug. "I like it as it is. I want to be able to wake up in the morning without worrying about coven hunters showing up on the doorstep. I'm really not planning to hurt anyone. I want to spend some of my days convincing werewolves that they really should get more comprehensive auto insurance. I want to find stolen artworks, lost fairy children, and magical objects. And if the coven wants me to keep doing odd jobs for them…well, I wouldn't mind that either. Not if they pay."

Rebecca sat there, not saying anything, until I almost thought she'd forgotten about me. With everything I could feel around her though, I knew that wasn't likely.

"It won't be easy," she said, after what seemed like an eternity. "I mean, you aren't the one who has to convince the coven of all this."

I stood, stretching. "I'm sure you'll do a good job. We both know that it's better than the alternative. Just say that I'm protected under the tolerance directive of the coven."

"What?"

"I'm a supernatural being. I haven't killed or harmed anyone. So really, I should be accepted into the coven as an associate member, with all of the protections and support that you give any werewolf, fey folk, goblin, and others who swear their allegiance to the coven, and further—"

"You're not really suggesting that I try to turn the coven's own words against them, are you?" Rebecca asked.

I shrugged. "If that's what it takes."

"But we both know that no one takes that directive seriously. It's just a way to make sure that none of the fey start attacking us."

"Tell them that you don't take it seriously," I suggested with a tight smile. "Then see how long that lasts. Of course, if you'd rather I presented myself as a witch…"

And showed myself to be twice as powerful as any of them. The coven might claim to be about the interests of all witches, but I knew from previously being one of the weakest in it that it was really about power. No one ever learned that truth as well as when they didn't *have* power.

"I understand what you're saying," Rebecca assured me. She looked at one of the paintings. Anywhere but at me. "You know it might not work out, though. They might turn around and say no, Elle. They might send me back to finish what I started. They might send more hunters like Evert."

"Well, at least you'd enjoy that part," I said. Like I said, I wasn't entirely back to being her friend.

"That…that isn't…"

"Fair?" I turned her back to me with a touch. "An entire life of being lied to isn't fair, Rebecca. So, I'll say once more how it is going to be. I'm going to get on with my life. I'm going to investigate insurance cases. If the coven is sensible, it won't get in my way. It certainly won't send assassins. We're *all* just going to get on with our lives. Live and let live."

Rebecca swallowed. "This isn't wise, Elle."

I let a flicker of fear touch her then. Not much. Just a reminder of what I'd done to her before. "It's possibly wiser than the alternative. And Rebecca?"

She shivered. "What?"

"If they do send assassins after me, don't be with them."

Rebecca hung her head. "I won't."

It was time to go. "Enjoy the new art exhibition, Rebecca. It's full of magic, if you only know how to feel it. Emotion, anyway. It's almost the same thing. Or it would be, if you understood."

Her mouth dropped open in shock. I left her like that—the spider waiting for a fly—and headed for the museum exit.

I would have preferred to extract a promise from Rebecca that the coven would leave Niall and me alone, but I knew things weren't that simple. Nothing in my life was likely to ever be simple again, even if it had been before.

I had a warlock-vampire for a boyfriend, and a whole side to my life that I still had to learn about and understand, not to mention the likelihood that no matter how hard I tried, at least some people would want to kill me over it.

I had memories of a mother who loved me very much, yet she had tried to protect me to the point where she put walls around me to stop me from becoming what I had to be.

I had a present life that had me feeling every emotion in the gallery as I walked through it, and a future that could contain just about anything. Up to and including one very beautiful male enchanter.

Niall met me outside the gallery, greeting me with a kiss that curled my toes inside of my shoes. I could put up with any number of meetings if there were kisses like that waiting after them.

"So," he asked, with a slightly bitter glance at the art center, "Is everything the way you want it now?"

"You're still annoyed about giving up the Escher woodcut of the letter A?"

"Maybe a little, but it was the right thing to do. But you know that's not what I was asking you."

I shrugged. "Everything with the coven and with Rebecca is…complicated."

"And you? What are you going to do now?"

That was the question I'd answered for Rebecca. For Niall too, more than once. This time, I supposed I owed him something more than vague intentions. He had kept his end of the bargain over the paintings, after all. And the near-priceless Escher.

"I have the hundred thousand from the insurers. I guess I'm going to need to rely on G&P for jobs more often, because I can't imagine the coven will come back to me with more work referrals…not any time soon."

Niall nodded. "We can but hope."

"Anyway, I was thinking that the money might be best used acquiring a proper office." Rather than just running everything out of my house, the way I normally did. "That might let me acquire a few jobs from the public. The less normal parts of it, at least."

"That sounds like the kind of thing you might need help with," Niall said.

I laughed. "Are you offering?"

"Me? Haven't you heard? I'm far too busy seducing repressed coven witches and masterminding art theft plots for real work."

Not to mention running the business that kept him in fine art and nice suits.

"You're right. I probably do need help on my cases. I can think of one place I might get some."

"Really?" Niall cocked his head.

I smiled. "I know a werewolf lawyer who is looking to move closer to his mother. He sort of owes me a favor, too. I was thinking of giving him a call. Of course, that might make things more than a little interesting around the full moon."

Niall grinned at that. "Well, that's all right then. I know you like things complicated."

Did I? I thought about the stark simplicity of my home, then about my job, Niall, and all of the rest of it…

I kissed him. "Complicated has its moments."

The End

***

Elle and Niall will return in
Witch and Famous
(The Witch Detectives #2)

About the Authors

Eve Paludan is a mystery and romance writer who lives on the west side of Los Angeles, California. She also edits for bestselling authors.

Stuart Sharp is a writer, ghostwriter and historian based in East Yorkshire. Having dabbled in urban fantasy, he currently writes comic fantasy.

Made in the USA
Coppell, TX
27 November 2021

66535662R00090